Fractured
Threads

Fractured
Threads

Stories
by

Michael J. Vowles

First published in Great Britain by Michael J. Vowles, 2022

First Edition 2022

ISBN: 978-1-3999-3221-9

Some of these stories first appeared in slightly altered forms in the following publications: "Shane Lives in Allouez Now" in *The Writer's Playground* and "Hamza's Loon" in *Ripple 2022: A Kingston University Student Anthology*.

Cover design & illustration by Jasmine S. Higgins.

Typeset by Michael J. Vowles in Garamond.

For Sofia

Contents

Shane Lives in Allouez Now

Before he left, my daddy filled my head with images of inferno. Pine trees exploding. Men boiling alive as they hid inside a water tank. High winds whipping up tsunamis of fire 200-feet high, rolling over towns and farms with extreme prejudice. It must have been screaming followed by total silence, I thought. A brutal end to all things.

When I asked why Peshtigo was so bad, Daddy smiled at me with closed lips. He said that I was a very clever girl because I always wanted to know the *why* more than the *what*. I didn't care that the temperatures reached 2000 degrees, or that over two billion trees were lost. What I wanted to know more than anything was why it happened.

We moved past the plaque, shivering a little and keeping our hands inside our scrunched-up coat sleeves. It was cold but bright. I was wearing an old Packers coat that Daddy wore in the 1980s when he was my age. It was still too big for me but that's part of why I loved it. I thought that if I kept wearing it, I would grow into the spaces he left for me and become him.

"Slash-and-burn. You know what that means?"

"No."

What I loved about my trips with Daddy was how he didn't treat me like a 12-year-old. He spoke of insatiable consumption, how men set fires everywhere to clear the forest for farmland, and the metaphor inside the swirling tornado of flame that came to punish them. It was difficult to keep up with all of it, but I felt the images taking root in my brain.

Inside the mill there was a display with a horseshoe that had been warped by the fire. I said it looked like a black snake. Daddy said it was a warning, but he didn't say for what. Perhaps he was just being silly. But I've tried to interpret it in various ways since. That day was the last trip we took together for the year. After that the museums closed for the season. Snow fell with noiseless abandon over the streets. I didn't know it then, but there wouldn't be any more trips with Daddy to the forest.

A week before Christmas, I overheard him telling my mom that it was possible to love two people at once. When they realized I was there, they told me to go back to bed. The next morning Daddy was gone.

I learned straight away that it was difficult for my parents to be honest with me about what happened. Mom seemed to be constantly wrestling with the temptation to say what she really felt, denying me answers whenever I had questions but blurting out vague remarks laced with bitterness whenever I was silent.

It was a shit Christmas. I didn't see Daddy again until the new year. He said he hadn't planned for things to happen this way, which told me that he had, in fact, planned for things to happen.

"I wanted to give you one last Christmas as a family," he explained, as though expecting praise. I stared at him and he quickly averted his gaze. I knew in that moment that I was a problem Daddy was trying to disentangle himself from.

Before, I had always felt that he belonged wholly to me. This was in spite of the fact that he was rarely available. I assumed he was always off doing something fantastic. But when he came home, and when he took me on our daddy-daughter dates to the forest, I felt like I was in full possession of everything he had to give. It was inconceivable- from the way he spoke, the way he acted, the way he looked at me- that there could possibly be room for anything else in his life but me. Now, all of a sudden, he could barely look me in the eyes.

When I think of that time, I think mostly of silent car journeys. A nauseating, wordless gulf between us that made our trip to Peshtigo feel like a long time ago- even though in reality it had only been a few short months. He dropped me off and didn't get out. In fact, he didn't even wait to see whether I made it inside the house or not. By the time I reached the door, his car was out of sight. One time, a friend of mine who lived across the street asked me why he never got out of the car.

"He must be so busy," she said, brushing clumps of snow from her eyelashes.

"Shane lives in Allouez now," I said. I'd stopped calling him Daddy to counteract the way he had stopped treating me like an equal. Where before he had engaged my imagination, now he spoke in an unfamiliar, formal tone with contrived questions about school, about what I was eating, about Mom. Mostly he seemed interested in trying to justify why he had left us. No matter what he said, I didn't say anything

11

back. I knew that he found my silence irritating, because out of nowhere he would snap at me about whatever he could think of. That my hair was too long, that I was slouching, that my grades were slipping. I didn't care. I remained silent and Shane would sigh, as though it were me that had changed.

When the snow began to melt, Shane told me that I had a little sister. We were parked outside an Applebee's in De Pere. I didn't know what to say but he kept staring at me. I looked out the window at a family leaving the restaurant. My eyes followed them all the way to their car and lingered on the parking spot after they had gone.

"Well?"

"What?"

"Don't you have anything to say?"

"No."

"Hey, look at me when I'm talking to you," Shane said. I looked at him. There was something in his frown that felt to me like acting. "You know your attitude stinks," he said. For some reason I laughed. I don't think I meant to. Maybe I did.

Shane didn't seem to know what to say. This didn't surprise me- I had come to think of him as not very fantastic after all.

"Listen," he said after a long pause. "I know this isn't easy for you. But you should know your family, Kelsey."

At that moment he undid his seatbelt. I felt my chest tighten.

"Where are you going?" I said. But I knew. I could see it in his eyes. "No," I said.

"Yes."

"They're not."

"Yes, they are, and we're late."

I spun my gaze toward the restaurant windows, but I couldn't make out any of the faces inside.

"No."

"Come on. It's been three months already...it's time you met them."

"I'm not coming."

"Yes, you are."

"No, I'm not."

"Get out of the car, Kelsey!" Shane screamed. I really didn't want to, but I started crying. Shane sighed. "Please?"

"No."

"So you're just going to sit here this whole time? Because I'm not driving you home."

I didn't say anything. Shane looked completely lost. The man I used to know had always been in control. Or so it had seemed. Now all I could think was how weak and pathetic he looked. He was clearly weighing up what to do. Then, when he committed, it was in a flash; he grumbled something like "Fine," and got out of the car. He didn't close the door properly, so he doubled back and slammed it shut. I braced myself, imagining this new, erratic version of my father dragging me kicking and screaming out of the car, but he walked instead to the front door without looking back.

For the next few minutes, I sat there crying. I didn't even notice when she came out of the restaurant. A tap on the car window snapped me out of my daze, and all of a sudden I was face to face with a woman and a baby. The woman motioned with her free hand for me to roll down the window. I recognized her from my father's office. Jessica something. I wiped my eyes and rolled down the window. It wasn't lost on me that the baby was at least a year old. It also wasn't lost on me how long it took to make them. I started doing the math in my head but gave up when a pudgy hand extended itself towards me.

"This is your little sister, Morgan," Jessica said, beaming at the child. She didn't feel the need to introduce herself, or ask why I was out here crying. For a second, I thought she was going to pass Morgan through the car window, but she just shuffled closer so that Morgan could grab a tiny handful of my hair. I guess that interested Morgan for some reason. She turned the blonde locks between her fingers and examined them. I just looked at her, trying and failing to find any resemblance to myself.

After what felt like a long time, Jessica said, "Why don't you come in?"

I didn't have the strength to argue. As much as I didn't want to accept her authority over me, it was difficult to give attitude to a grown-up I didn't know. We went inside the Applebee's and joined Shane at a table, who looked to me like he was sulking. Jessica caressed his shoulders with her free hand before strapping Morgan into a highchair.

"She's getting so heavy!"

Jessica did most of the talking. Shane didn't say anything until it was time to order. "Look, Kels, they have wings," he said. It was clear from his voice that he was expecting this statement to be a big win, as though my mood could be so easily manipulated. Buffalo wings were my favorite food on the planet. When Shane and I used to go on our trips to Door County, to Devil's Lake, to the Chequamegon-Nicolet National Forest, we would always stop for buffalo wings. But that was then.

"I'm vegan now," I blurted out.

Shane cocked his head. "No, you're not."

"Yes I am."

"Since when?"

"Since February."

14

Shane couldn't prove that I wasn't. He hadn't been around.

"Do you even know what a vegan is?" he asked. "Because it's not the same as a vegetarian."

"I know that," I lied.

I ordered fries and picked at them disinterestedly. Shane looked miserable the whole time. Jessica seemed determined to maintain a smile. When Morgan started crying, Jessica tapped my father on the arm and said, "Could you?"

Shane got up and carried my baby sister to the restroom. Jessica turned her fixed smile on me.

"Not hungry?"

"Nope."

"Your father loves you, you know," she told me, leaning close. "It's important you remember that. This is hard for him too…"

As Shane drove me back home in silence, I thought about what he had told me in Peshtigo. Maybe he had been trying to warn me after all. Maybe, I thought, he had to burn our family down for his new one to grow.

*

I committed to veganism for the next four years just to spite Shane. I hated it, but I couldn't give him the satisfaction that he was right about me. Plus, I seemed to be going through a phase where I wanted to make myself suffer.

Shane began spoiling me with gifts and doting on me with compliments, but I made sure never to thank him. My feeling was that he didn't want me back at all. What he really wanted was for me to absolve him for what he did. And as much as I wanted things to go back to the way they were, my instinct was that I had to keep denying him anything that might be construed as forgiveness. That way, he would be tied to me forever. If I forgave him, he would be free to leave me behind and focus on his new family. That's what he really wanted- to unburden himself of the past. I wouldn't let him.

For example, when I was fifteen, I got a septum piercing. I knew Shane would hate it, but he couldn't say anything. I got a piercing in the shape of a horseshoe, to remind him of our last daddy-daughter date when I was twelve, although I'm not sure he picked up on that. He just winced when he looked at it.

I also got myself a boyfriend- Austin- who I liked to emphasize as the main man in my life. He was a sweet, shy boy who had been pursuing me since middle school. When I finally accepted, I let him know straight away that I was broken.

"Don't hurt me," I warned him. Austin said he wouldn't. I made him promise. "You can't ever hurt me like Shane did."

Austin came to understand that whenever I told him he was nothing like my father, this was to be taken as the highest compliment. I said this to him for the first time at Bay Beach during a period of breathless silence after getting off the Zippin' Pippin'. We stood on a boardwalk and watched a line of Canada Geese crossing the bay. Austin hugged me and it was nice.

He wasn't much of a talker, which was maybe why I liked him. But I knew how closely he paid attention, because for my birthday he presented me with a book on North American old growth forests, which he had signed with his name on the contents page. I felt bad because it seemed quite thoughtful, which made me suspect that Austin thought we were further along than I thought we were. Shane and Jessica gave me a $100 gift card for Macy's. The truth was I had outgrown a lot of my clothes in the past year, but I didn't want to use their money, so I gave it to Mom, who then ended up buying me clothes anyway. So, whatever, I guess.

I didn't bring Austin to my mom's house the way I did Dad and Jessica's. Mostly because it had become a depressing place to hang out. There were plenty of men that came into my mom's life prepared to love her, but the problem was that she didn't seem prepared to let them. She put little effort into anything that might make her happy, and I thought that maybe I was the same way.

Because of what happened between Shane and Jessica, sex disgusted me. This was another thing I made Austin understand early on. There would be no sex. I let him kiss me now and then, mostly when he had made me happy. It was like a reward. We always held hands when I dragged him along to Shane and Jessica's house in Allouez. I played with his hair when I knew Shane was watching. Even though sex repulsed me, I still wanted my father to think that I was having it, to keep him in the dark about my life as much as possible.

For his part, Austin seemed to have little capacity for hatred. Even though I'd told him again and again about how Shane had degraded my mother, how he had kept his family in Allouez hidden from us for as long as he could, how he had hoped to somehow have the best of both worlds, Austin was always polite to him in person. And he loved my kid sister. Every time we went there, he would play with her until she exhausted herself from laughter. It was obvious that he just had so much love to give. But this realization only made me feel shitty about myself. His well ran much deeper than my own. We would leave Shane's house in silence, and Austin would ask me what was wrong.

"Nothing," I would say. That's when I first started lying to him.

By the time I was sixteen, I started smoking weed to feel better about myself. I had a part-time job at the Dairy Queen in De Pere where I became infamous for my "resting bitch face" at the drive-thru window. A coworker two years older than me, Bryan, could see that I was unhappy. He started offering me lifts home, and then he started offering me other things. We would park down the street and get high in his car, where I could forget about the father who betrayed me, the mother who had grown absent and bitter, the boyfriend who pedestalized me, and the little sister who had stolen everything. Pretty soon getting high was all I wanted to do.

Then one time, I was having a laughing fit in Bryan's car, when he reached over and grabbed my boob. I was shocked. No one had ever touched me there. He worked up to a rough massage over my polo shirt and asked me if I wanted him to stop.

I got home quite late that night, unsure of how to feel. My mom didn't even say anything. I wanted her to ask what I had been doing because I was aware of a pain between my legs and blood on my underwear. It was becoming more and more acute, but I was still so high, so I decided to shower.

When I woke up the next day I cried. I told Mom I was sick and she let me take the day off, which I spent wrapped up in bed. There was only the ticking of an unseen clock. It was as if I were waiting for something to happen that would restore the status quo. But the reality of what I'd done only seemed to harden, setting in like a fresh coat of paint. I guess it turned out that I was more like Shane after all. It was all I had ever wanted when I was younger. In the afternoon, Austin called me to ask if I was okay. I told him what had happened and he hung up. I cried some more. It was the most I had cried since that day at Applebee's years ago.

I decided to call Shane when he got home from work.

"Is everything okay?" he asked.

"Can we go to Wequiock Falls?"

"Uh, sure. You mind if your sister comes? Jess is out."

"Sure."

He sounded worried but cautiously happy. I had never once called him before or asked him to hang out.

Twenty minutes later, they were outside.

"You still have this?" Shane said, gesturing at the old hand-me-down Packers coat.

"Of course."

"I haven't seen you wear it in years."

The truth was I had asked Mom to throw it out the day I got back from Applebee's. But it turns out she had kept a hold of it, even at the height of her anger towards my father. Despite how much I had grown, it was still too big for me.

At the falls, Morgan raced ahead. It felt good to be in the forest again. Shane asked in a low voice if I was okay. I started to cry, even though I had spent the whole day crying in bed. I liked that when this happened, his first instinct was to hug me rather than press me for details.

"I'm sorry," I told him. Even though it wasn't him I had hurt, I felt like we were somehow morally even.

"I'm sorry too," he said. We stopped for a while, and he held me close. He kissed my forehead and rubbed my back. "I'm so sorry," he said.

Up ahead, Morgan was transfixed by the falls. From my angle, it looked like a perfect photograph, with her off to the side, balanced on the rocks, looking up at the tumbling waters with her mouth half-open.

"Let's keep her like this forever," I said.

The Apartment

From a place somewhere between sleep and waking, he reached for her in the humid dark. The dreaming hand rested on her love handles, that soft part of her waist that she was insecure about but that he found endearing. Depending on her mood, she either felt self-conscious when he touched her there, or she found it cute. Presently she made no reaction whatsoever, and he wondered if she was asleep after all.

He wasn't entirely sure whether he was awake himself, or how long it had been since they had gone to bed. There was just the total blackness of the room, the rise and fall of her hip anchoring him to the real world. Maybe he reached out to vanquish the fear that he wouldn't find anything there. He would rather the tiniest light could be left on to prevent that disorientated, weightless sensation, but he knew she didn't like it.

"Mm?"

"Mm," he answered her.

"Are you awake?" she asked in a small voice. It was a valid question. He was a restless sleeper, and even before the air conditioner gave out, he had a tendency to reach for her in the dark.

"Can't sleep," he said.

"Mm," she answered.

It was a thick darkness, prickling at their skin, and so they had taken the comforter out of the sheet and just kept the sheet. It coiled stickily around their ankles, apparently having been kicked gradually downwards since they had gone to bed. It had been almost a full day since they had lodged their maintenance request with the front desk but no one had arrived yet.

He shuffled closer to her, until his body was up against hers and his lips brushed her ear lobe. She remained on her side, facing away from him. He waited a second before sliding his hand from her hip and toying with the buttons of her pajama shirt. Not undoing them, just running his fingers up and down from button to button to introduce the idea that he might. When she didn't react, his fingers slid up to her collar and he popped the top button.

"It's too hot," she said then, and he retracted his hand, first to her hip and then off of her body completely. A cumbersome silence lay in its wake. She stayed as she was, and though he couldn't see, he was sure her eyes were closed shut. He waited for her to say something else, though he wasn't sure what exactly. When she didn't, he inched away on the mattress and lay on his back.

He lay like that for a while, until his lower back started hurting again and he rolled onto his side, facing toward the window. He knew by now that he wouldn't be able to fall asleep before it started aching again and he would have to shift position once more. His eyes burned with wakefulness, and it seemed like each time he opened them, the world got clearer. The lines of the window asserted themselves. No light passed through the venetian blinds, which told him they were nowhere near morning yet.

The window faced east, towards the gulf. When they had first moved into the apartment in January, the bed had been underneath rather than parallel to it. He remembered that first day, their bodies aching from the back and forth hauling of furniture up the exterior staircase, how the two of them had sat on their knees and gazed out at the parking lot below. A line of palmettoes inside an iron fence blocked a potential view of the bayou.

"A room with a view, can't complain about that I reckon," he had said.

"Yeah, we can see all the raccoons scurrying over the garbage skip," she gushed in mock-excitement.

"Still a view," he said. "Better'n the last one I had."

He was aware that the new place was a step up for him but a step down for her. He had been living in the guest bedroom at his aunt's house in Friendswood, whereas she had rented a four-bedroom apartment with her friends in Upper Kirby. Even split between the four of them, she had been paying more for that place, with its open concept and smooth linoleum floors, than she would be renting this apartment with just him.

"You get what you pay for."

"Speaking of…" he said, and started bouncing on his knees. They had decided to get a brand-new mattress to go with the new apartment.

She started bouncing alongside him, looking down at their new purchase. They kept their hands on the windowsill for balance. It was a lot less firm than the one he had been sleeping on at his aunt's house. That was something he hadn't even thought about when they had decided to move in together. Picking a mattress that was optimal for two people with different sleeping preferences.

He bounced harder and she giggled.

"Are you thinking what I'm thinking?" he said.

"Torchy's?" she gasped, grabbing his arm. Her eyes were wide and it looked like her glasses were about to fall off of her nose.

"Troll."

"What do you mean? Were you expecting something else?"

When they were finished, they lay for a while on the new mattress, facing each other. They had not even put on the sheets or pillows yet. It was quite soft, but he thought he could get used to it. Above them, a fan cooled their panting bodies.

"You owe me Torchy's," she said eventually, and reached up to turn the fan off by the hanging string.

That was almost seven months ago, although it felt longer. Impossibly longer, he thought. He stared upward now at the emergent lines of the string in the dark. Presently the fan blew hot air on their sleepless bodies. It wasn't nothing. But it wasn't much, either. Groaning, he sat up, pulled on the beaded string, and waited. Nothing seemed to happen. Since they had moved the bed, the fan was slightly off-center, and he had to lean over her to grab it.

"It doesn't go any faster," she said. "You just turned it off."

Sure enough, after a few seconds, the blades stopped spinning. Then air laid upon them like a prickling blanket.

He pulled the string again, then once more to get the fan's full speed. He was careful not to lose his balance and fall on top of her in the dark. When the fan started up again, he lay back down, this time on his back. The pain was just above his tailbone. He lifted up his hips and rubbed the area with his knuckles, groaning.

It occurred to him then that that time on the fresh mattress seven months ago, the very day they had moved in, was the last time they had been together. He didn't know what that meant, if anything. Maybe it was just something that happened when you approached thirty. What he did know was that it hadn't felt like the last time. He recalled a kind of restless energy about their movements, the way they didn't have to keep their noise in check for thought of his aunt or her roommates. A newness, as though the change in bed had opened up all kinds of possibilities. Since that day they had started once or twice but never finished. There was always an off-ramp that she took before things went too far. Most of the time, he tried not to think about it. Sometimes he couldn't help it.

Just then a coughing fit snapped him back to the present. He angled himself away from her, leaning almost off the side of the bed, and covered his mouth with his hand. The jerk in movement sent a sharp spasm of pain down his spine. The cough left behind a dry tickle in his throat and he knew that in a few seconds, it would come back. He rolled out of bed and entered the bathroom, closing the door behind him.

She was used to it at this point. For her, there had been few symptoms. A loss of taste for a few days. Not even a dry cough. For him, it seemed like every symptom he could get, he did get. Even though they were both positive, he slept on the couch so that his coughing wouldn't keep her awake. The coughing was the worst of it. They had both been negative for a month now, but for him the cough persisted in random outbursts. Not only that, but he felt like his lung capacity had been permanently handicapped. They had read online that some people had labored breathing for months after contracting the virus.

"I don't understand," she had kept saying, shaking her head.

"What's there to understand?"

"Like, are you high-risk? Do you have some underlying condition?"

"I don't know."

"So what do we do?"

"We follow the CDC guidelines and wait for it to fuck off, I reckon."

He knew that that answer wouldn't satisfy her. Her eyebrows seemed frozen in a dramatic pose.

"What?" he snapped, coughing. She blinked at him, pushing up her glasses. Something about her expression was ticking him off. He didn't even know what.

"Nothing," she mumbled, her eyes glassy. Somehow that only made him more angry.

"It feels like you're yelling at me for being sick."

"Of course not!"

"That's what it feels like."

"I'm not. I'm just worried how we're going to pay the fucking rent if neither of us are able to work."

"I can't deal with you right now," he said, coughing.

Looking back on it, he wasn't even sure why he had been so mad at her. He held his head under the faucet, drinking cold water. When his cough had finally receded, he left the bathroom out of the other door, into the main room. Still no light outside. He felt his way to the kitchen and stopped finally at the fridge. He opened it, flooding light and cold over his torso. It was a welcome reprieve, much better than the fan.

He gazed down at himself. He was wearing pajama shorts and a white tank top. Before they had moved in together, he had always slept naked. She'd told him once that she had never slept naked in her life. Maybe that's why he had switched. It would have felt weird to him if one of them was naked and the other wasn't. She hadn't asked him to wear pajamas, but he decided to start wearing them nonetheless. Seemed like something thirty-year-olds did.

As he basked in the chilly light of the fridge, he cleared his throat. That damned cough. During the worst of it, he had been completely bedridden. More than once he had woken himself up with a particularly bad coughing fit.

Why the virus had struck him so violently and not her, he had no idea. He didn't have a history of being sickly, or suffering from fevers. And yet it had left him so helpless. She had held a cold compress to his forehead while he lay there coughing into an old rag, feeling like the couch that was still so new might actually become his deathbed.

When she finally left his side to go into their bedroom, he thought about how lucky he was- despite how wretched he felt. She was everything that had been missing in his mother. It wasn't just her actions during those awful two weeks- making him chicken noodle soup, stroking his hair, putting on his favorite movies, bringing him cups of ginger tea and boxes of ibuprofen- it was the whole vibe she gave off. Relentlessly energetic. Endlessly patient. Doggedly upbeat, despite having the virus herself. She had hidden how exhausted she was. It wasn't something he was used to. Even his aunt- much as he loved the woman- had never tended to him like that.

He closed the door of the refrigerator, turning instead to gaze at the fading outline of the couch where he had been more or less confined for a fortnight. It was much cooler out here than in the bedroom. He made his way carefully through the darkness and lay down as he had used to on the couch. He sank into the fabric and felt the memory of those godawful two weeks press into his skin.

Blurred days of half-sleep and painkillers. Days that felt long at the time but seemed short in retrospect. Days that started with him gazing at the bedroom door, waiting for her to wake up. He thought about that now as he lay facing the outline of the door in the dark. Every morning was the same. He would wake up in a daze, just as the first light slanted down onto his body, his temple throbbing, his throat dry, a sharp pain in his lungs when he drew breath. Just gazing at that door, willing time to fast-forward to the moment she would emerge.

The relief when she did.

Every agony she must have felt, she internalized. She put everything on hold until he was better again. Even when she called her family, she tried to sound upbeat when he was in earshot. He didn't understand Spanish, but he paid attention to the inflections of her voice. With his eyes closed he would follow its sound as she paced around the room, talking about who knows what. Even though he didn't understand, he liked listening to the energy in her voice. It was different to when she spoke English. More expressive. Before they had moved in together, he had never actually heard her speak her native tongue. Her using it around him felt like an intimacy, like he had been inducted into her private life.

He closed his eyes then and tried to imagine her holding the cold compress against his forehead while she chatted in animated tones to her mom on the phone. It wasn't something he had imagined missing at the time.

Slowly but surely, he had gotten better. The headaches were the first to go. The coughs became less frequent. His energy returned. And when it did, hers lapsed.

"When are you going back to work?"

"I don't know," he had answered, tapping his thumbs intermittently on the PS4 controller. A pause. "Maybe I won't."

"You can't just sit here playing video games all day."

He sighed, keeping his eyes on the screen.

"So what are you going to do?" she pressed.

He sighed again and told her about the research he had been doing into cryptocurrencies and NFTs.

"I bet I could make more money through passive income than I would at the damn warehouse," he added, unable to look at her dumbfounded expression.

"Why did you never tell me about any of this?"

"I thought you'd freak out."

Looking back on the summer, it was no surprise to him that isolating had hit her harder than it had him. He worked in a shipping warehouse for a multinational e-commerce company and she was a flight attendant for a major airline. When he tested positive, he had gotten two week's paid leave. But even when he was negative again, he was still too weak, too much at risk. *Long Covid*, he had heard some people call it online. It had been two months and he still felt knocked out. The warehouse couldn't take him back, and she was put on furlough by the airline.

Being tied to the ground had been refreshing for her at first. She started reading again. She finally tried the baking recipes she saved on Pinterest. She played *Among Us* and *Fall Guys* with her cousins in Costa Rica. But the longer it went on, the more agitated she got. He thought back to a conversation they had had almost two years ago, at the La Madeleine in Tanglewood.

"There are three things you need to know before you start dating a flight attendant," she said, leaning on the table with her elbows and holding up three fingers. "One: our Instagram feed makes our lifestyle look better than it actually is. Two: we're gone half the time and crew scheduling can assign us flights on hella short notice. And three: when we actually are around, we're usually exhausted."

His hand reached across the table, closing over the upheld fingers.

"Are you even listening, you cheese?"

He grinned, turning her palm over and caressing it with his thumb.

"God, this is a mistake, isn't it?" she said, rolling her eyes.

"It'll be fine. I don't want you around all the time anyway," he teased.

Presently, he picked up his cell phone and opened up Instagram. Her last post was a black square, June 2nd. Before that, you had to go back to March. Past there the feed became weekly, brightly-colored posts of cocktails, sponsored bikinis, and infinity pools. Every week a new hotel, a new beach, a new landmark. No wonder she was depressed, even if the whole flight attendant gig wasn't as fun as it looked from the outside. The sooner she was back in the sky, the better.

He didn't think he would miss that distance from her either. From the bathroom he heard the toilet flush. He looked up at the door connecting it to the main room, but she didn't come looking for him. She must have gone back to bed. He turned his gaze instead to the closed door to the bedroom, thinking back to those mornings he used to lay there waiting for her to open it. It was no doubt cooler for her without him in the bed. She would be laying there now, closer to the center, but still facing the far wall. Not making any sound. She never did. She slept silent, still, and deep. He thought about the shape her body made on its side, and the empty space around her. The ceiling fan ushering in a dreamless, untroubled sleep.

As for himself, he lay on the couch until the first suggestion of light appeared behind the blinds. Gray, tropical stands fell on the door and brought out its color. They crept in further, revealing the green of her succulents, the black of his PS4, the dark orange of the couch. The soft brown of her grandma in the framed photo hanging on the wall. The chestnut brown of the linoleum floor. Grays of unwashed dishes on the coffee table, on the counter. Myriad grays in the dust on their television.

When she woke up, he would have to find a way to tell her what he knew he had to.

Sometime before daybreak, he heard a rustling in the next room. He waited for the bedroom door to open, but after a few seconds she came out via the bathroom instead. Her hair was in a dry, messy bun that reminded him of a bird's nest and he could see the deep marks her glasses left on the bridge of her nose. She pinched the front of her pajama shirt and tried to shake out the heat. She stopped on the other side of the coffee table, her sleepless face hiding nothing.

"We need to talk," he said.

"I know."

It was as good a time as any, he thought.

"Maybe we should go back to being just friends," he said.

Neither of them looked at each other. The gray light continued to seep into the apartment and illuminate the possessions they had bought together. A whole set of stainless-steel silverware from Target. Hand-sanitizer, face masks, and ibuprofen. An uncarved pineapple. The denim jacket he had bought her for Christmas, slung over a chair at the breakfast table.

"Okay," she said, nodding. "I think so too."

"I can sleep out here, give you some privacy."

She looked at him then and he wondered if he had hurt her.

"You don't have to…it's not like anything is gonna happen…"

"I prefer it out here anyway," he said.

She nodded. Maybe she didn't have the strength to fight. Maybe she just didn't care.

For a while they remained frozen, not knowing what to say. The gray light reached the curve of her hips, her shirt collar, her septum piercing, the ends of her jet-black hair. All things now inaccessible to him. He averted his gaze, as though to preserve her dignity. After a while, she turned and soundlessly shuffled toward the bedroom door. She opened it and closed it shut behind her. It made a soft but definite sound.

He lay staring at the door for a while. It felt different now.

Morning light flooded into the apartment, and at last he drifted into sleep.

Hamza's Loon

Out on the lake a pair of loons rounded the nearest island. They made their way across the lake side by side. Sometimes they dove beneath the water when they spotted a leech or a crayfish, but the couple always reassembled itself.

*

At the end of the dock, Cameron Bauer watched his father cast a line into the water. It was a lousy spot at mid-morning, but Cameron knew that Jackson wouldn't stop fishing it so long as it offered him a distraction from everything else. Seeing this, he hesitated before interrupting him.

"I think they're here," he said. Through the trees came the familiar sound of churning gravel as a car descended the uneven forest road.

"I know. I'm not deaf yet," Jackson grumbled, bobbing the lure in the water and remaining where he stood. Cameron lingered behind him, putting his hands in his pockets before taking them out again. He glanced over his shoulder in time to see his sister's car slowly emerge from the trees.

"Why's she bringing him along anyway?" Cameron said. His father tried to look like he was concentrating on the line. "I mean- don't you think that's weird?"

Jackson sighed, reeling in the lure.

"You know Aubree. She's got her own process."

Cameron made a *tsch* sound with his tongue and teeth. "I don't know if it's much of a process."

"Come on," Jackson said. "Let's go say hi. Your sister's gonna need us this weekend."

By the time they made their way up the log steps to the flat grassy area beneath the cabin, Aubree was already out the car.

"Where is everybody?" she hollered.

"They went to the Mennonite store to pick up some things for tonight," Cameron yelled back. He stopped for a second and looked at her. All the tiny differences in her appearance he attributed instantly to what had happened to her. There was definitely a weight gain- now she was pear-shaped with wide hips. Probably comfort-eating, Cameron thought. Though whether that was the grief or the monotony of the pandemic, he wasn't sure. Probably both. It seemed only yesterday she was a champion swimmer in high school.

At that moment Aubree dropped her bags and ran straight for him. He put his hands up to stop her, but before he knew it her body crashed into his and she flung her arms around his neck. She was shorter than he remembered.

"Hey, hey," Cameron said, trying to shake her loose. "What about social-distancing?"

"I don't care," Aubree said. "I've missed you."

"You too, Aubs," Cameron said, lifting her arms steadily off his shoulders.

"Relax, Cam," Jackson said as he reached the grass. "We're gonna be sharing the cabin together for the weekend after all."

Aubree squealed and hugged her father.

"Did you get a Covid test at least?" Cameron asked.

"Oh shoot, I forgot!"

"Great," Cameron said. Aubree hadn't changed too much then. He turned to see a man with close-cropped hair and an oval face making his way over the grass. It really was Bryan Steuck. Cameron couldn't believe that he was here after all these years, on this weekend of all weekends. His sister was full of surprises but this one really took the cake. He wondered for a brief moment if he and Bryan would admit to remembering each other or act like strangers.

The first thing Cameron noticed was that Bryan's face looked almost exactly as he remembered it. The only difference was the way he was wearing it. He approached them with an openness that Cameron found annoying. You would think he'd look embarrassed or awkward, given the occasion. But he walked right up to them and stuck out his hand for Jackson to shake. When Bryan turned his eyes toward him, Cameron almost jumped.

"Hey Cam," he said with an easy smile, as though he came up to the lake all the time. Cameron made sure he was positioned well out of handshaking range. Bryan's hand instead found the small of Aubree's back, as though it settled there often.

*

Bryan joined Aubree out on the deck, where she stood admiring the view of the lake. Her hair was tied up in a bun, but the breeze caught a few strands in a way he liked. For a second he watched her. Aubree seemed a lot more relaxed now that they were finally here.

"Hey, *you* can't be nervous," Bryan had teased her back in the car. "They're *your* family. How'd you think I feel?"

"I'm not nervous," she protested.

"Liar."

The Bauer cabin was built into a hill that poked out of the forest, the various levels of the property connected by a series of wooden staircases that zig-zagged up and down the escarpment. So far only Aubree's brother and father were here. The meeting had gone well enough, Bryan thought. A little stiff maybe. But this whole weekend was destined to be awkward.

"My parents built this place, you know," Aubree said.

"No way."

"Way. Thirty years ago, this hill was nothing but forest."

They went around to the side, where Bryan stopped to admire a little rock garden tucked against a corner of the building. On the neat bed of innumerable, smaller stones were arranged six large, uneven rocks with flat sides facing up.

Each rock had been hand-painted with a different color combo, and on each one was written a different name. The left two rocks (orange-blue and red-yellow) belonged to the two men he'd just met, Aubree's father Jackson and brother Cameron. The right two (blue-white and pink-purple) read Taylor and Heidi, who he knew were Aubree's sister and mother respectively. Bryan focused on the middle two however, which seemed closer together than the other rocks. The green and yellow one was Aubree's. The other, red and white, belonged to Hamza.

"Neat," Bryan said, gesturing at them.

"Oh yeah," Aubree said, as though she hadn't noticed the stones in a long time. "Yeah, we all picked out our stones from the bottom of the lake."

"I like it."

Aubree glanced at them for a second before drifting away. A rumble of tires on gravel emerged from the pines and she shrieked, running over to greet the car that was arriving. Bryan followed in her wake. As he rounded the corner of the cabin, Cameron came out of the door at the same time. Both men flinched. Bryan opened his mouth to make a joke out of it, but Cameron quickly averted his gaze and strode off toward the exterior staircase.

Three women had exited the car and were all hugging Aubree, who was squealing again. Heidi and Taylor looked vaguely familiar to him, though Bryan was sure he had never actually spoken to them. The third, a sturdy, dark-haired woman, he could infer was Lizzie- Cameron's steady girlfriend.

Bryan wondered if the Bauers usually greeted each other this effusively, or if a special case was being made for Aubree. Then again, he reminded himself as he watched from the top of the steps, none of the Bauers had seen each other since the pandemic started. For some of them, it might even have been as far back as the funeral.

When Bryan went down to make his introductions, the usual two-meter pandemic etiquette resumed- for which he was grateful. He had already shaken Jackson's hand out of habit. Or perhaps to show some kind of primitive deference.

"I remember you," Taylor said. "Your mom worked in the school cafeteria."

"That's right," Bryan said. "She doesn't work there anymore though."

They decided to go out on the pontoon boat. Aubree told her father she was eager to give Bryan a tour of the whole lake. Jackson headed down the staircase that led to the dock, while Cameron, Heidi, Taylor, and Lizzie carried the grocery haul up the one that led to the cabin. Aubree and Bryan stayed on the middle level.

"Are you always this extra with your family?" Bryan asked as she slid her arms around his neck.

"What do you mean?" Aubree said, pouting at him.

"Nothing, I was just teasing."

"Good. I'm glad you're here…"

Aubree leaned up and they kissed. The two of them held each other for a few moments before Aubree announced she was going to see if her dad needed any help with the boat. Bryan felt a prickle of sweat on the back of his neck. Turning around, he looked up at the deck just in time to see Cameron shuffle away.

*

As the day went on, Bryan became aware of a recurring pattern in the group conversations. Everyone- except for Cameron, who gave him a wide berth- was polite toward him, but none of them talked to him for as long as they could help it.

Questions came with little to no eye contact, and there were never any follow-ups when he answered. With each other, the Bauers talked heartily, but never about anything that Bryan felt like he could contribute to. They would rise in tempo and then suddenly drop, as though they had just remembered he was there. It was a cycle of organic excitement followed by lulls of self-consciousness.

At first Aubree made several attempts to include him, but by the afternoon, even she was barely talking to him. With the others, however, she spoke breathlessly. Bryan thought he noticed everyone's eyes linger on Aubree long after she finished talking, which made him wonder if she had always been this hyperactive. Cameron paid particular attention to her, as though she were something crooked he wanted to fix.

Cameron Bauer. The youngest of the three siblings. Younger than Bryan, though he couldn't remember how much younger. There was little that he remembered of Cameron. A wide forehead and a small chin. Taller than he expected, but no meat on him. Pale skin that blushed at the slightest thing. The only thing that Bryan really remembered were his eyes. Blue, nervous eyes that suggested a tendency to preempt a perceived threat.

Jackson tied the pontoon to the tree of a tiny island in the middle of the lake and some of them went swimming. Even though it was a hot day, the water was cold. Taylor and Aubree were laughing as they recited a story about Cameron climbing a tree but finding himself too scared to either jump into the water or climb back down. Bryan lay on his back, away from the rest of the group, and closed his eyes as he floated.

A year ago in northern Minnesota, his Great Uncle Aarsvold had led him through the pouring rain at night and into a barn. There, he had told Bryan that he would be dead within ten years if he carried on living the way he did.

"You're thirty now. Time to grow up. It doesn't matter what you do; you just have to try *something*."

After that, Bryan spent several months sleeping on his brother's couch. In January, he landed his job at the digital marketing agency and soon after got an apartment in town. When he first saw Aubree Bauer at her desk, it took him a few seconds to recognize her. She didn't look like Bryan's old lab partner, the girl who had surprised Bryan by not being afraid of him. And he- what had he looked like to her at that moment? Nothing like the kid that everyone had worshipped in middle school.

It was only two months later, when the agency split the staff into alternating weeks of remote and office work, that the two of them realized they were both damaged. After that, things happened quickly. Long conversations in an otherwise empty office led to unbuttoning her blouse on his couch. When his brother phoned him, he remarked how Bryan sounded happier.

"It's like the world had to go to shit for you to thrive," he joked.

Presently, Bryan thought about his brother's words as he felt the sunlight rest on his eyelids, and heard the sound of Aubree's laughter over the water.

*

That evening Jackson put together a fish fry while the rest of them drank Spotted Cow and played card games on the deck. Bryan, who had gone back inside to change out of his swim shorts, hesitated before re-joining them. So far, he hadn't spent much time in the cabin itself. It was an eclectic place, in which no amount of space seemed unoccupied.

Of the many things that vied for his attention, Bryan was drawn most of all to a series of paintings along the walls. A white-tailed deer, a muskie, a bald eagle. Tamarack swamps and old growth forests. A side view of a loon, as though drawn for a premodern field guide. Bryan stared into the lidless blood-red eye and felt something like nausea. Despite this, he couldn't look away.

A toilet flushed nearby. Seconds later, Heidi emerged from a door down the hall. When she looked up, she seemed startled to find Bryan lingering there.

"I'm sorry, were you waiting to use the restroom?"

She didn't look much like Aubree, Bryan thought.

"No, no. I was just admiring these paintings here. Who's the artist?"

Heidi blinked, turning to look at the wall. There was an audible intake of breath when she did. She started nodding, gazing at the various scenes of rural Wisconsin and its fauna.

"Yes, they are nice," she whispered, continuing to nod as she inspected them. "These are all Hamza's work."

"Really?" Bryan exclaimed. "They're amazing."

Heidi smiled at that, as though it were her own son Bryan was complimenting. It felt like the first genuine smile he had gotten out of one of them.

"Yes, they really are."

"Are these all scenes from this lake?"

"Yes. Hamza really loved it up here."

"I can tell."

There was a pause. Heidi cleared her throat.

"Did...you know him?"

"No," Bryan said. "No, I never knew him."

Heidi nodded once again, slower this time. She glanced back at the loon in front of them, before taking a deep breath.

"Excuse me," she said, and headed for the deck. Bryan stayed with the paintings a while longer. Outside he could hear Aubree laughing hysterically at something. Rather than

41

going out to join them he went into the bedroom where he and Aubree had left their bags. There were only two bedrooms in the cabin, but it seemed like it had already been assumed that he and Aubree would take one. Naturally, Jackson and Heidi would take the other. That left Cameron and Lizzie the fold-out mattress and Taylor the couch. He recalled Aubree saying something along the lines that this had always been unofficially hers when he'd asked about sleeping arrangements.

He realized then that it was probably because she and Hamza had used it so often over the past ten years. His eyes fell on the bed. Bryan thought about all the times Hamza must have woken up in these sheets with Aubree in his arms, the sunlight on his face.

*

Bryan heard the door to the deck slide open, then close again. An aggressive burp reverberated around the cabin, and he followed the sound into the main room, where he found Aubree in a fit of giggles.

"Oh *shit*," Bryan said. "How many beers did you drink?"

Aubree stumbled toward him, still trying to contain her laughter.

"Why are you hiding in here? Hm? I think *that's* the real question."

"I'm not, I was just admiring these paintings. Your mom told me that Hamza made them."

"Oh, those…" Aubree said, not even glancing at them. "Yeah…he was really talented."

"I don't have any talent."

"Me neither," Aubree said.

42

"Hey, you're supposed to say: *everyone has a talent.*"

"Not like Hamza did."

"Clearly."

There was a silence between them that went on too long. Aubree frowned.

"Is something wrong?"

"No. Are *you* okay?"

"I'm fine," Aubree said. Another long silence. Neither of them looked at each other. Bryan focused back on the red eye of Hamza's loon. Among the growing shadows, it looked menacing.

Aubree stepped closer, swaying ever so slightly, until her nose touched his chin. "Do you wanna...you know..." she purred into his ear.

"*Jesus!*" Bryan hissed, checking over his shoulder that no one else was in the cabin. "Has your mind touched the void?"

"Come on..." Aubree said. "I want you."

"Aubs, your family is right there."

"I don't care. Come on, let's go back to the room..."

"No way," Bryan said, stepping out of reach. "What's wrong with you?"

Aubree's face changed in an instant. At first, he was worried she was going to cry. Instead, she remained very still.

"What's *wrong* with me?" she said, raising her voice.

Bryan opened his mouth to speak just as Cameron came in the side door.

"That's enough alcohol for tonight. You need to drink some water."

"Hey," Cameron snapped. "Don't tell her what to do, man."

Bryan winced. He knew that Cameron Bauer had been waiting over fifteen years for this. Seeing him standing there in the open doorway, nostrils flaring, cheeks flushed, Bryan remembered. *Think fast, asshole!* The pigskin had launched straight for Cameron's unsuspecting face. At the last second, he looked up. And out came the tooth.

Everyone in the hallway exploded in laughter. And worse, Cameron would be teased for the gap in his teeth for a whole year.

"It's okay, Cam," Aubree assured him. Cameron remained in the doorway, the fist that held the handle shaking. "Really. I'm so shitfaced."

Cameron continued to glare at Bryan for a few more seconds before turning on his heel and disappearing down the exterior staircase. Bryan sighed.

"I should talk to him."

"You should," Aubree agreed. She staggered, balancing herself on a brick column in the center of the living room. Then she said, "I came in to tell you we're getting ready to release Hamza's balloons."

"Do you need me?" Bryan asked. Aubree didn't answer him. "Maybe it would be better if I sat it out. Let you be with your family."

"Right."

*

Bryan found Cameron sitting on the dock. Back up on the deck, the Bauers prepared the balloons. They were all bright colors. Heidi was insistent that, if anything, it was a celebration. Hamza would have been thirty-two that day.

44

The sky was a soft, sunless gray. The trees now seemed to join together in a singular dark print against the pale evening. The sun was gone, but its light lingered on the water's surface.

On the lake, the loon now made a lonesome silhouette. Uncoupled, it simply bobbed in the water, not knowing whether to swim or to fly.

The Layover I

I saw her first in the restroom mirror, applying a nude lipstick. I made a short, closed-mouth smile at her reflection and she froze in place for a few seconds. As I washed my hands, I could sense her mouth hanging open. When she finally collected herself and returned to applying the lipstick, she said, "Thought you went back to school."

"I did. I mean- I have. But then-"

"Crew scheduling?"

"Right."

We were silent for a few moments. Carmen put away her lipstick and considered her reflection for a minute. I cleared my throat.

"How have you b-"

"This your first flight since Corona?"

"No, I worked right at the beginning for a while," I said, neither looking at her nor my reflection. "But it's my first flight since being furloughed."

"Welcome to the shit," she smirked.

Now neither of us were doing anything with our hands. We were just standing there, me looking down at the sink and her gazing at her reflection. I noticed that Carmen had a new uniform. I was wearing the same dark dress buttoned up from the hem to the collar, a blue scarf for color. Carmen was wearing a pressed blouse tucked into a navy-blue skirt, with a matching navy-blue cardigan slung over her forearm. The blouse was the lightest shade of blue with a simple checkered pattern. She looked gorgeous. I thought about telling her this but I decided against it.

The flight had more passengers than I expected, but nowhere near what it used to be. My body slipped back into the unconscious rhythms of the cabin as though the past six months had been nothing but a hazy dream. As if nothing at all had happened in that time, when the truth was, everything had happened.

Being a flight attendant was a multitude of little actions. And with each one, I could feel a cautious confidence growing inside me. I felt it in the balls of my feet as I marched down the aisle, in my hands as I shut the luggage compartments, and in my voice as a tone I hadn't used since March reasserted itself effortlessly. But there were new actions that broke the old rhythm- and kept my confidence in check.

I had been briefed on the new health and safety protocols, and tried to ensure they didn't sap my sense of authority. It was something I had been fretting over on the drive down to O'Hare- that I'd enter the plane and find that I'd lost my adult self for good. That I'd be the little girl I'd reverted to during furlough, and the passengers would be able to see it right away. I thought about the little girl I'd been this summer, that had lost so much weight, that bit her nails, that had discovered more and more threads of her hair were falling out. I'd spent my furlough back in my mom's house in De Pere, in the bedroom I'd grown up in that hadn't changed at all. The apartment I'd shared with Carmen in Houston felt like another life.

For the most part, the passengers accepted the health and safety protocols. Some were a little bumbling and flustered about it, but they didn't look at me and see a little girl who had spent most of the summer in her pajamas. Make-up works miracles, I guess. My nerves settled with the passengers' compliance. I became a woman again.

Then, somewhere over Quebec, a man in cargo shorts decided that wearing a face mask was a violation of his "Amendment Rights". Which amendment, he wouldn't say. I'd heard about this phenomenon already, through viral Tik Toks and the horror stories of my friends that were still working over the summer. While the mistreatment of airline staff was nothing new, this particular scenario presented an interesting challenge to the dichotomy that lay at the heart of what we did. In short, I had my professional self and my real self, and I had to keep them divorced for as long as we were in the sky. I couldn't let the real me show herself to the passengers, no matter what happened.

On the adjacent aisle I could see Carmen trying hard to maintain her professional self. When the man started to get belligerent, and I felt the agitated grumble of the other passengers around me, I wheeled around to Carmen's aisle, not really knowing what I was going to say. I'd dealt with drunk or abusive passengers before, but now I was rusty. I had been my real self for too long, and as my quick footsteps brought me to Carmen's side, I was worried who might slip out.

"Sir...*sir*..." I said until he acknowledged me. "My colleague has asked you nicely several times to respect our company policy. If you won't put your mask back on, the captain will have to turn us back around to Chicago. Is that what you want?"

He looked at me like I was joking. I was close to letting the real me slip out.

"This isn't a conversation. Put it back on or we'll turn this flight around."

I waited for him to accuse me of bluffing, but he reached back in his pocket for the mask, shaking his head.

"Fuckin' ridiculous," he said.

"Thank you," I said, making it clear I wasn't saying that as my real self.

A moment later I found Carmen in the galley. She was standing with her hands on her hips and seemed to be taking some deep breaths. We shared a quick look before I returned to my aisle.

London was the first international layover Carmen and I had ever taken, back in 2018. We were just a few months out of flight school and neither of us had ever been to Europe before. Looking back on it, it seemed like we barely slept the whole time. We took a tour of Shakespeare's Globe and stopped for lunch at a place called Pieminister at Carmen's giggling insistence. Everything felt spontaneous and a little silly. Carmen got a septum piercing after having long admired my own. I filmed the moment the tiny puncture was made in her skin. She laughed the whole time, and we took a selfie afterwards to show the world we were twins. That night we went out for drinks and Carmen ordered a pint of Guinness.

"That's not British, that's *Irish*," I told her.

Carmen made a face like I was being unnecessarily pedantic.

"Whatever. It's still going to taste more authentic than if we ordered it in America."

We spent the night dancing with British guys that weren't at all like Hugh Grant. They threw their elbows around to mark their territory and kept leaning in to yell slurred gibberish in our ears as though it were prized gossip.

I remember on our last day we went to The Notting Hill Bookshop before taking our purchases over to Holland Park. Carmen bought an illustrated copy of *Little Women* and I took a chance on a new paperback called *The Overstory*. I thought this was an interesting contrast. Carmen had chosen a story she knew well, and I had purchased something based on gut instinct. We both admitted to having loved reading as teenagers despite never having finished a book in years.

"There's just no time," I agreed. "Or at least, it feels that way."

While we did get free time, the life of a flight attendant was so stop-start; any progress we made on a good book would get interrupted when crew scheduling came calling. And they could call us up at any moment. By the time we were free again, we would have lost touch with the characters and the plot. All rhythm would be wiped clean. Not like either of us tried very hard. Whenever we weren't working, we were under a quilt binging Netflix and drinking wine. Being a flight attendant was especially exhausting, but we both agreed that we wouldn't change it for the world.

I remembered how we sat in silence for a while, gazing at how pristine and lovely the books looked in our laps. We were both hoping, I think, that the excitement of going to The Notting Hill Bookshop together would give us the extra motivation we needed to get back into reading.

"It's the great guilt of our generation," Carmen said. "I swear. When millennials look at books, they feel guilty, even if they never liked them all that much in the first place."

I replayed this memory in my head as we took our seats for landing. I'd finally gotten around to reading my copy of *The Overstory* while on furlough. It was the first book I'd finished since high school. I looked across at Carmen, strapped into the jumpseat and gazing at her shoes, and wondered if she had ever touched her copy of *Little Women* after that day in Holland Park two years ago. I imagined her packing up her things when she moved out of our Houston apartment, and what she might have felt when she set eyes on the book again.

Guilt?

By the time we got to our hotel, I felt an inexplicable sense of energy coursing through my body, demanding to be used. It was like I was so tired I'd come out the other side. I flopped down on the bed, making a starfish of myself in the sheets. Two years ago, Carmen and I would have been sitting cross-legged on the mattress, browsing through TripAdvisor on our phones. Now she was a few doors down. Maybe sleeping, maybe getting ready to go out, but certainly not thinking of stopping by. I lay there for a while, zoning out, until I heard my belly growl.

"Oh jeepers," I said aloud, even though no one was there.

I took a quick shower, changed into jeans and a flannel, and went down the road to a quirky burger joint. It was bustling with people, even though it was 10pm. I ordered a chicken burger and fries, enjoying the ambience with my copy of *Girl, Woman, Other*. No one came up to me, and I didn't approach anyone myself, but I still felt like I was being social. I didn't want to go back to being alone in my room. When I finished my food, I tried to sit there and read for a while longer, but I couldn't concentrate. Snatching up the book in a flash of movement and returning it to my handbag, I decided to leave. My restless feet took me back down the street to the hotel where I found a few of the cabin crew in the hotel bar. Carmen was with them, sipping on what looked like a gin and tonic.

I put on my brightest smile and joined them. The bartender asked me what I wanted, and in a sudden flash of inspiration, I ordered a Guinness, looking over at Carmen in the hope she'd crack a smile. She didn't seem to notice. For the most part she just sat there sipping intermittently on her drink, her eyes wandering around the bar but not seeming to really focus on anything. Now and then she nodded or went "Mm," in acknowledgement of what was being said.

For my part, I chatted breathlessly, trying my best to tempt her into conversation without addressing her directly. The others couldn't match my energy, however, and twenty minutes later they got up to leave.

"Goodnight, Wisconsin," one of them said to me, squeezing my shoulder affectionately as she turned away.

Carmen and I remained at the bar, which is what I had been hoping would happen. She kept her eyes in every direction except mine, and seeing this, I let the silence hang there for a while. Then, clearing my throat, I said, "Hey, I'll get the next round."

Carmen glanced at me but didn't say anything. I caught the bartender's eye and he came over.

"I'll have another Guinness, and she'll have…"

"I'll take a daiquiri," Carmen said.

"Actually, me too," I said.

"So two daiquiris?"

"Yes."

We watched him make the cocktails in silence. We were still silent when the drinks came. Carmen started on hers straight away while I stirred mine with the straw, frowning at it.

"It's good to see you again."

Carmen swallowed. "You too."

"How's Nate?"

"Actually, we broke up," Carmen said. I opened my mouth but she cut me off. "It's okay. We both decided to go back to being friends."

"I'm sorry," I said. Carmen didn't say anything. "So, did he go back to his aunt's place then?"

"No. We still live together. Our lease is up in January. It's fine."

We lapsed once again into silence. The two of them had moved into that apartment just two months before the pandemic began. I remember wondering if I was part of the reason why they had moved in together so soon in their relationship.

"Why…" I paused before saying it. Carmen could probably tell what I was going to ask from my tone, so maybe I was just giving her a few seconds to brace herself, or even to run away. I gulped. "Why did we stop being friends?"

Carmen let a few long seconds pass before answering.

"We didn't stop," she said, looking down at her drink.

I knew she didn't believe what she was saying, so I gave her time to answer me truthfully. We sat there in silence for five minutes, then ten, then twenty. In that time, we finished several more cocktails. The fact that Carmen had stuck around told me that I was going to get an answer eventually. After what must have been half an hour, Carmen's lips appeared to be loosening. They oscillated in the imitation of speech while I watched her. I tried to keep my composure but I was starting to feel a little drunk myself.

"It's not that we *stopped* being friends," Carmen said. "It's just that-"

"We were so close."

"It's just that we stopped overlapping."

"No, that's not it. You hate me."

"I don't hate you, Kelsey."

"I've always had this fear that it's always a matter of time before people start to hate me. It's like, the more I show of myself to them, the less they want to be around me. I can't get close to anyone, because once they get to actually know me, they become repulsed."

"That's toxic as fuck."

"It's true though. I thought you would be the one to break the cycle, but it eventually happened with you too."

"No, it didn't," Carmen said, turning on her barstool so that she was fully facing me. I was aware that the bartender was listening to this whole thing, pretending to clean a glass, but I didn't care. My head felt light. "I don't hate you."

"We were best friends. But I just don't know how to make anyone like me. I don't know how to *be*, if that makes sense. I try out all these different versions of myself, but they never work. Can't you just tell me like...like...what kind of person to be, to get people to like me?"

Carmen frowned at me. I swayed a little but kept my eyes locked onto her own, pleading for a response.

"God, you're so self-centered," she finally said.

"What?"

"That's your problem right there. You're trying to be what you think other people will like, instead of just being yourself. It's counterproductive."

"Nothing seems to work," I said, returning to my straw even though I'd already finished my drink. I swallowed melted ice with little to no trace of the cocktail.

"This is middle school behavior," Carmen said.

"I've always felt like I'm still a kid. Like, my brain still operates the same way it did when I was fourteen, I swear."

"You just..." Carmen began. She hiccupped. "Shit, I don't know."

"No, tell me."

"No, it's nothing."

"I can take it. I want to grow as a person. Just tell me, what's my worst trait?"

"That's such a self-centered question," Carmen said. "Honestly. No one is perfect. There's not some easy fix that I can give you that's going to change your social life. I know that's what you want, but it doesn't work that way."

We were quiet for a while. It seemed like there was no other sound in the hotel bar, and to be honest there really wasn't. Just an older couple in a corner booth, drinking quietly, and the poor man behind the counter, acting like he couldn't hear us. I was in a state of knowing I should be embarrassed but not being able to feel it. I caught the bartender's eye and he blushed, turning quickly away.

He pities me, I thought.

"But we were best friends for two years," I said.

"Yes, you've said that."

"You said we stopped overlapping or something."

"Yes."

"How does that happen?"

"Shit, I don't know. People change."

"No, they don't," I said. "You just got sick of me. It's like I said- everyone does, eventually."

Carmen growled with the back of her throat. "Fuck, Kelsey. We were best friends and then we weren't. So what?"

"I just want to know why."

"*Honestly*," Carmen said, her perfect little eyebrows raised high on her forehead, "You can just be a little too much, okay? You're hella dramatic and, okay, that's just who you are. I kept telling myself that, but every little thing you did annoyed me, and then I'd feel bad for feeling so annoyed, because it's just who you are. You're *extremely* extra. And that's an understatement. So, I just started to keep my distance, because it didn't feel fair to tell you that just being around you was driving me crazy."

Abruptly, Carmen stopped herself. It was like she had run out of air.

"I see," I said.

"Look, don't feel bad or anything-"

"Thanks for being honest," I said.

Neither of us said anything after that. A few seconds passed before Carmen slipped off her stool and left the bar. I remained there for a while longer. I didn't order another drink. I just sat there thinking about what she had said. The bartender walked over.

"That wasn't very nice," he said in a small voice.

I ignored him and left the bar. As I walked up the stairs, I thought about the last few months Carmen and I had lived together in Houston. How much more cheerful Carmen seemed to be around other people- around everyone, it seemed, but me. How she gradually stopped inviting me to stuff. The silly argument we got into at the 2019 Houston Pride Festival that neither of us seemed to understand.

Yeah, but you've never struggled. Not like us.

I'm not saying I have.

Yeah, but you wish you had. You romanticize it. You love surrounding yourself with us. You hate how white and suburban you actually are.

I stopped outside Carmen's door. There was no sound inside. I thought about the last photo taken of us, by our friend Terrell just a few weeks before the airline put me on furlough. We were sat on the patio at Baby Barnaby's, mimosa flutes in hand, turned toward each other and laughing with our eyes scrunched shut. The photo looked like it belonged to a time earlier in our friendship, as though the two of us were keeping up appearances for Terrell. The photo had gotten over a hundred likes on Instagram. Our flight attendant friends had commented things like "I love y'all's friendship", "Soul sistas", and "Y'all are so darn cute".

I had felt a naïve hope when reading them that it was a sign things might return to the way they used to be. But I cringed too, thinking about what Carmen might feel when she read them.

I continued walking down the corridor and entered my room. As I lay on the bed, I opened up Instagram, went over to Terrell's profile, and scrolled back to February when the photo was taken. I looked at it for a long time. We really did look like best friends, like we had been caught right in the midst of a joke that only the two of us would find that hilarious. There was no clue in the photo- which had 142 likes and 24 comments to be exact- that I was, fundamentally and incurably "too much". The photo was a curated truth. I tried to lose myself in that truth, staring at it for a long time in the dark, feeling my eyes sting. I stared until my eyes watered- until, at last, I collapsed into sleep.

The Layover II

As the bus rattled through Wimbledon, I checked her profile again. The first photo showed a curvaceous woman in a flight attendant uniform, posing in a mirror. In the second she wore a black sports bra and gray sweatpants, her hair in a messy bun. She wore big, thick-rimmed glasses and both her arms had a full sleeve of tattoos. This time she looked directly at the camera with an unimpressed expression, her mouth in a thin line. The third, and last, photo showed the woman drinking out of a coconut in an infinity pool. The woman wore a revealing one-piece swimsuit. My eyes lingered for a second before I turned the phone over in my lap and checked no one behind me was looking, feeling my cheeks flush.

The city was a brick labyrinth of off-licenses, hair salons, and kebab shops. Every street seemed to end with a boarded-up retail chain. More people hopped onto the bus, and I adjusted my face mask. Sometimes I held my breath when people came near me, even though I knew it was foolish to think it made any difference. I didn't know shit about how airborne viruses worked.

It would be a while yet before the bus reached the stop. I checked the woman's profile again, scrolling down from the photos and re-reading her bio.

Coffee, tea, or me? Looking for a man to ruin my life. No Gemini pls.

I couldn't help but smirk. The app let you fill out prompts. One of them was "My personal hell is…" to which she had answered "Writing these fkn bios". She was witty, but in a deadpan way I didn't expect from an American. Not that I knew shit about Americans either.

My phone buzzed.

Are you sure this is a good idea?

It was my brother. Always was something of a do-gooder. I could tell him he was growing into our father, but I didn't fancy a fight before something like this.

I can't stay indoors forever. Virus might as well pwn me right now.

I'm not saying you shouldn't go. Just saying you gotta accept the risk and live with it, he replied.

Or not, lol.

Knob.

The truth was that I had messaged him this morning because I wasn't sure it was a great idea or not. Though I'd never admit as much, I trusted Harry. My brother was informed about this sort of thing. Had he told me definitively that it was unsafe to start dating again, I might have actually listened to him. But he hadn't, so I stayed on the bus.

Had I told him this girl was a flight attendant, of all things, he probably would have told me not to go. But I guess I omitted that detail. A few minutes passed and Harry sent a follow-up message.

Have fun bro.

That was that. I was definitely doing this. My feeling was always that any decision was better than no decision. When you committed, you doubled-down and didn't look back. I never permitted doubts to live in my head for very long. If there's one thing I didn't want people to see when they looked at me, it was my father. Always fretting over the road not taken.

I opened up WhatsApp then and checked the last conversation with my father.

Your mother and I have sent you some money for living expenses. Please check that the transfer went through.

I'd replied with a thumbs up.

Any word from the pub? Have you started looking for other jobs, just in case?

That one was five days ago. I hadn't replied yet. Dad was convinced I should have a contingency in place in the event the pub went under. But I was still getting furlough money right now. I didn't want to ask my boss how business was going. The fact they didn't need me back yet told me everything.

I stared at the conversation thread with my dad.

Not yet, I started typing. Just then he came online and I stopped. I stared for a few more seconds before deleting the text and closing out of the app.

At the next stop I alighted onto the street, keeping my mask on as I headed for the tube station. I realized then that I hadn't used the underground since the pandemic began. I hadn't had the need to go anywhere before today. As the escalator took me downward, I felt the familiar damp smell of the underground filling my nostrils, and I had this sense that today was the day I rejoined the world at large. Maybe that's why Harry had given me mixed feedback on using the app again. He knew I'd been stuck in the same miserable little room this whole time, fixed to my computer.

Today would be like waking up from hibernation, I thought. The tube carried me into central and every time someone coughed I damn near flinched. Everyone else seemed a little on the twitchy side too. The doors opened and people spilled out onto the platform, scattering as fast as they could toward the stairs. Before I knew it, I was above ground again and I could finally remove my mask. I took a moment to inhale the fresh air, before checking her hotel on Google Maps. It wasn't too far.

I followed the blue dots on my screen and ended up at a street with several large hotels. Fancy ones too. Doormen, valets, everything. According to my phone I had arrived at my destination. Just as I looked up, a woman coming the other way, also staring at her phone, walked right into me. My feet came to a stop, but it was too late. Warm coffee from a disposable cup splashed onto my shirt and the woman let out a little yelp of surprise.

"Oh my god, I'm so sorry!" she gushed.

I looked down at my shirt. It wasn't a big stain but it stood out against the light blue of my button-down.

"It's okay," I said. The truth was it was less than ideal.

"Shit, I totally ruined your nice shirt," the woman said. I noticed then that she was American. You couldn't mistake her for anything else really. She had a loud, energetic voice that you imagined Americans having. For a moment I just stood there and looked at her face. It took me a good few seconds to feel confident that this wasn't her. From a distance I might have thought so. But the face was different to the one I had seen in the photos.

Luckily, she didn't catch my dumbfounded stare. She was too busy rubbing the stain on my chest with her shirtsleeve.

"It's okay," I said again, trying to sound cheerful. "Seems like both of us were reading something important on our phones."

"Jeez, I'm such a klutz," the woman said. "I'm real sorry about that. You weren't heading to a job interview or something, I hope?"

The woman seemed determined to rub as much of the coffee from my shirt onto hers, but all it did was make both dirty.

"A date, actually."

She stopped when I said this and looked up at me, her eyes widening.

"Shit! I'm like, *so* sorry," she said. She realized then that she was still holding her hand in its scrunched-up sleeve against my chest, and withdrew it quickly. "I mean, you still look cute. It'll give you something to talk about."

"All I need is my smile," I said, flashing her a grin.

"You're right on the money, there. It's a wonderful smile."

"Thanks."

The woman smiled back at me.

"Well, don't keep them waiting!" she said after a few awkward seconds, making an exaggerated gesture of stepping aside and ushering me on my way.

"Right. Have a good day," I said, reminding myself how to put one foot in front of the other. We parted ways with a little nod to one another and I started up the wide steps toward the hotel's double glass doors. The doorman glanced at my shirt but didn't say anything. I was somewhat worried about the stain, but the shock of the warm coffee splashing suddenly down my front had given me a strange kind of confidence. In a way, the little encounter had energized me. It felt good to be holding conversations with strangers face-to-face again. And like the woman had said, maybe the whole business would end up breaking the ice.

I crossed the hotel lobby and entered the bar. It wasn't hard to find her. The place was empty except for a young woman sitting at a small table. She was sitting sideways in the chair and scrolling through her phone. I wondered how long she had been waiting. As I approached, she looked up and gave me a soft, shy smile. Within a second her eyes dropped to the stain on my chest. I smiled back, though it felt less natural than the one I had just given on the street outside.

"You must be Carmen," I said as she rose from her seat. I had wondered if I should open with a hug, but my muscles seized up as I reached her. Her body language was closed. I adapted, stopping a respectable distance away from her. I put my hands in my back pockets, trying to look as open and laid-back as possible.

"And you must be Sebastian," Carmen said. She studied the stain on my shirt. "You sure know how to make an impression, Sebastian."

"Yeah, that's my bad. It happened just now, right by the front steps. Wasn't looking where I was going and neither were they. Next thing you know I've got hot coffee all over me. You can call me Seb, by the way."

"I prefer Sebastian," she said, still examining the stain like it might be a problem. She was wearing high-waist jeans and a black lace camisole, so you could see all of the tattoos that covered her arms. Finely-trimmed eyebrows and long lashes. Straightened, shoulder-length hair, black as obsidian. A soft, dark-red lipstick. Leather boots. "What a shame. I like this shirt on you."

"Thanks. Bought it myself."

Carmen twisted her lips, as if to tell me she appreciated the effort but I'd have to do better to get a laugh out of her.

"Well it's too late to do anything about it now. Let's get out of this place."

The hotel was ideally situated to explore in any direction. We set out toward The British Museum and I could feel the coffee stain drying out in the post-summer heat. As Carmen and I made our way through the crowds of people, I wondered how the scale of the bustling city was making each of us feel. It probably had a different context for each of us, depending on our experience of COVID-19. It was definitely weird for me. I looked at her.

"How has pandemic been for you?"

Carmen took a moment to consider her answer.

"Shit."

"Ha, I can imagine."

"I was still working for the first few months, then I was furloughed for a while, and now I'm back. It's just been one big shit-show from the beginning."

"Have you had it yet?"

"Covid?"

"Yeah."

"I have. It was bound to happen with my job. I got it in the summer and ended up giving it to my ex. He's high-risk, which is why I got furloughed for a while. For me it was fine. Like, I didn't feel anything. But he had it real bad."

I thought about this new information. The fact that she had had the virus relatively recently meant I would probably be alright.

"How about you?" Carmen said.

"I haven't had it yet. I'd probably know if I'd had it, right?"

"Probably."

"I doubt it anyway. I've been furloughed since March, so I've only left the house to go shopping."

"Oh wow," Carmen said. "Doesn't that drive you crazy?"

"It does," I said. Our experiences of the pandemic were probably polar opposites. She had seen it up close- not just the virus itself, but the structural changes, the safety checks, the hysteria. All of it, I imagined. For me, it had always been remote. It existed mainly in news headlines and graphs. "It's actually the first time I've been out and about like this since the pandemic began."

"At some point you have to, I think," Carmen said, adjusting her handbag on her shoulder. "This is just the new normal."

"I agree. I've had enough of sitting in my room. If I get the 'vid, I get it. I don't care anymore."

Carmen nodded and we walked in silence to the end of the street. When we turned the corner, The British Museum came into view.

"I've never actually been here," I said.

"I have."

"Oh, really?"

"Sorta. Kinda. Ish. My first layover was in London, a couple years ago. My friend and I came too late, so we only got to see, like, a couple rooms before it closed. I've always wanted to come back."

We crossed the road and put on our face masks. I just had one of the blue disposable ones, whereas Carmen had a black cloth mask with "BLM" written on the front. Wearing the mask brought attention to her long eyelashes and I thought that she had probably always had guys chasing after her. With every little action she took that day, every look she gave me, every bit of information she disclosed, I would continue to update my impression of who she was. It was a fast-moving thing, the imagined image constantly shifting, constantly acquiring detail. But no matter what happened, I knew that by the end of the day, the image would be left incomplete.

I thought back to our conversation that morning on the app.

In town for a day and looking for someone to explore the city with. My layover ends tomorrow.

Fine by me. I'd downloaded the app again after the end of lockdown because I wanted a distraction. Any distraction would do. It was different going into something knowing it had a very definite expiry date, especially one so soon, but maybe that was a good thing. Nothing would be complicated this way. Nothing misunderstood, nothing to interpret. We would both have fun being tourists together, at a time we really needed it, and then go our separate ways.

It was a win-win, really.

Inside we stared up at an Easter Island statue and Carmen retrieved her glasses from her handbag. I offered her a mint and she accepted it, asking me, "So how much of this did y'all steal?"

"Most of it," I answered.

"So it's not a very *British* museum then, is it?"

"Not really, no. It's cool shit though," I said, smirking. One of the things I had to gauge today was how much of a dick she would let me be. Presently she cocked her head but maintained a deadpan face. She turned slowly from the statue and drifted into the atrium. From there I followed in her wake, keeping a slight distance, until she wandered into the Assyrian stuff.

"I just don't like that people have to come all the way here to see their own heritage," Carmen continued. I'd never thought about it before. We stared at an obelisk depicting a king receiving tribute before drifting apart. She stopped at some cuneiform tablets and my feet took me to a stone statue of a bull with wings and a man's head. I admired it for a long time. There was a strange kind of quiet in the museum. Just the cumulative echoes of footsteps and hushed voices. After a while, she came up beside me and squinted up at the mythical creature.

"That's pretty sick," she admitted.

"It's a Lamassu."

"What does it do?"

"Guards things."

"Like what?"

"Important things. So don't go creeping about."

"Nerd."

"I'm just saying. You might be cute, but you don't want to mess with an ancient guardian spirit."

"You're such a Nimrud," Carmen said, turning on her heel. I gazed at the bearded face of the statue for a moment longer before it dawned on me what she had said.

"Hey, now who's the nerd?" I called back to her.

She pretended like she hadn't heard me and slipped out of the room. I found her again in the atrium.

"We're never going to be able to see all of it, are we?" she said.

"What do you wanna see?"

"I want to see if any of my culture is here."

"Alright. What is your culture?"

"I'm from Costa Rica."

"I thought you were American."

"Naturalized. I was born in Costa Rica and lived there until I was, like, seven years old. Then my family emigrated to Texas."

"Interesting. Do you ever go back there?"

"Almost every year. All of my extended family is in Costa Rica."

"You must be close, to visit that often," I said.

"We're super close. I fucking love my family, but I haven't been able to see any of them this year because..."

"Corona."

Carmen nodded, her eyes wandering over the tessellating glass roof. Her arms were folded across her chest and she was angled away from me.

"Alright, so let's go find some Costa Rican stuff," I said. Her eyes met mine then and she angled herself back toward me. She was back from wherever she had gone to those past few moments. "I'm interested. I don't know anything about your culture."

"I'm half-indigenous," Carmen said after we set off. "But I don't really know anything about my indigenous side. So that's what I want to see."

Eventually we found ourselves face to face with a stone sculpture of a man with a club in one hand and a severed head in the other. The sculpture had been excavated in the Nicoya Peninsula, Costa Rica. We examined it in silence. It struck me then that we were gazing into the eyes of her ancestors. Maybe that was why she had fallen silent. Even though she was right next to me, I knew that she was far away. Unreachable, maybe.

The man's face seemed borderline friendly, the lips curled slightly upward in a soft smile, as though he were presenting the disembodied head as a gift. The head itself gave the impression that it wasn't quite dead. Maybe I'd been playing too much *God of War* during lockdown, but I imagined the severed head offering sarcastic commentary on the man's choices.

I was snapped back to the present when I felt Carmen's hand on my bicep.

"Let's move on," she whispered.

A pleasant kind of shockwave ascended my arm where she had touched it. We continued this pattern of drifting apart and coming suddenly together. Throughout the rest of the day, I felt like we were constantly orbiting each other closely, and at certain points we would converge, slotting seamlessly into sync.

As the museum was about to close, I headed for the shop and picked up a book on the Assyrian Empire.

"Go on, make fun of me," I said.

"No, I think it's cute," Carmen said. "You really liked that stuff, huh?"

"Yep."

"Still a Nimrud though."

We rambled throughout Leicester Square and Soho for a while, before heading back in the direction of Carmen's hotel. On the corner of the road was an organic burger restaurant that we had earmarked earlier. I thought that the design was very futuristic. By the time we sat down I was grateful. My feet were killing me, which I guess was a product of being trapped in my room all summer long. Carmen, on the other hand, didn't seem tired. She was probably used to being on her feet all the time.

The whole orbiting thing paused once we were sat down. Now we were sat across from each other, her eyes fixed onto mine from behind those large glasses, and her conversation was more pointed. She looked different somehow.

"You haven't told me anything about yourself yet."

"You haven't asked."

"I'm asking now."

"Alright. What do you wanna know?"

Carmen frowned at me. She paused, taking a sip of water, before leaning back and asking, "Like, what do you do? You said you were furloughed. Furloughed from what, exactly?"

It was hard to maintain eye contact with her all of a sudden. As lovely as those eyes were, they were low-key kind of intimidating.

"A pub. Well, a restaurant-pub."

"What do you do there?"

"I'm a chef," I said. That was my first lie of the evening. My actual job title was "kitchen porter", which was a more professional way of saying dishwasher. I spent most of my shifts washing dishes and scrubbing the kitchen clean after the chefs were done with it. That's why I was on furlough. Only a few essential staff- a bartender, a couple servers, and a chef- were currently working. Everything I usually did, they could do together. I was the least essential.

I hadn't planned on lying to Carmen, but I had also been deliberately keeping the conversation about her throughout the day. My feeling was that women liked men who were ambitious. I didn't like talking about myself because there wasn't really anything interesting to say. That's probably why my relationships never lasted very long. My ex-girlfriends looked at me and saw someone that wasn't going anywhere.

"Do you like it?"

"It's alright."

I felt bad for offering closed answers. After a while she stopped and we fell into silence. I was conscious then that

I had to reignite the conversation from scratch and build a new momentum. Talking about the here and now never interested me. I preferred to talk about tomorrows. Faraway things and faraway places. It wasn't that I hated my life; it's just that it was boring.

Our burgers came then, and the silence no longer felt awkward. Still, I wondered how long it would drag on. I was aware of the time, that she could leave at any moment. It was getting late after all. But I didn't want our date to end yet. I had to be interesting enough to keep her here. If the silence lingered, she would just remember her regular life and start prepping for her shift tomorrow.

"How is it?" was all I could think to say.

"It's good," Carmen said over a mouthful of beef patty.

"Good."

No momentum gained.

"When they make a vaccine and this pandemic ends, I'd like to go traveling again," I said. It wasn't strictly true, but it could be true. I *did* want to see the world someday.

"Oh yeah? Where do you wanna go?"

"Maybe I'll check out Costa Rica."

"A fine choice."

"Or Texas."

"Eh," Carmen said, tilting her head. Then she laughed a little. "It's got its pros and cons."

"Steak?"

"Pro, for sure."

"Jesus freaks?"

"Con."

"Weather?"

"Pro. If you can handle it."

"Rattlesnakes?"

"Con."

"You."

"Definite pro," Carmen said, grinning.

"Well," I said, finally able to maintain eye contact again. "The jury's still out on that one."

Carmen broke off a piece of her burger bun and threw it at my chest. It bounced into my lap.

"I'm a catch, I'll have you know," she exclaimed. Whenever she got animated, her eyes seemed to bulge out of her face. Maybe it was the glasses. I picked up the piece of bread from my lap and ate it. We stared at each other for a second. "You wouldn't be able to keep up with me anyway," she said.

"Nah, you're nothing I can't handle. I'm experienced."

"How experienced?" she asked, a mischievous edge to her voice.

"That's classified," I said. "But let's just say I know a thing or two about..."

"Crazy bitches?"

"You said it, not me."

"You couldn't handle my craziness."

"Only one way to find out."

Carmen popped the last of her burger into her mouth.

"Besides, dating a flight attendant isn't easy. There's a reason we're all crazy," she said. "You would have to be cool with your girlfriend constantly traveling, leaving at a moment's notice, not knowing where she is...or who she's with."

"I could deal with it."

Carmen laughed.

"They all say that. Every last one of them."

"How many are we talking?" I asked.

Carmen fixed me with that deadpan look of hers I was beginning to know well.

"Enough to make you feel very, very small."

A server came to take our empty plates.

"Doesn't that get lonely for you?" I asked after the server had left. "Sleeping in hotels all the time. Always on the move. Not letting anyone get close."

"Sometimes," Carmen admitted.

After leaving the burger place, we decided to go for drinks at a cocktail bar a couple of streets away. We walked in silence, but it was a pleasant silence. By now the last light had left the sky. There was only the din of faraway traffic, and the clapping of our soles together on the shadowed pavement. It was an unhurried, unified sound that told me she wasn't thinking of anything in particular.

The glass front of the cocktail bar was bathed in vibrant pink, and you could see the dark silhouettes of the people inside. We stopped in front of the entrance to put on our face masks and retrieve our IDs. A wall of EDM rushed out of the doors whenever the bouncer admitted someone, and as it hit me, I felt my father taking root in my body. There was no doubt that this place was riddled with the virus. But I couldn't let Carmen see my father. We shuffled closer to the entrance, and I felt a hotness gripping my chest.

"You good?" Carmen said, and my ears burned.

"Yep," I managed, my throat so dry the words almost didn't make it out.

Carmen was excited. She peered through the glass doors and bounced a little. I tried to look less stiff, as though I could shake my father out of my skin, but it was never that easy. I'd be alright once I had a couple drinks in me. I was thankful for the face mask. It helped conceal the nerves.

We got to the front of the line and Carmen went first. The bouncer glanced at her passport and let her in. Then she was gone. You couldn't see much through the glass doors. Just a nebulous mass of silhouettes, and the pink neon that lined the bar. It was the farthest I had felt from Carmen all day, and I was anxious for the bouncer to hurry up and let me in so that I could reconnect with her. He frowned at my driver's license and for a split second I wondered if I'd seen the last of her. But then he handed it back to me and I was let in.

The inside felt like something from a movie. Everyone was dressed up nice. All the women in dresses, the men in button-downs and chinos. It was a young crowd too, late twenties and early thirties. Some people were sat on leather couches, some at small tables, but a lot were standing. And not everyone was wearing a mask, either.

I shuffled past a group of people that I decided were probably law graduates and scanned the bar for a sign of Carmen. Just as I was beginning to panic, I felt her hand on my bicep again. A wave of relief passed over me and I wondered if she could see the gratitude in my eyes when I looked at her. She said something but I couldn't hear her over the music. Her eyes told me that she was laughing behind her mask, and she pulled herself up close to my ear and shouted something. I caught the word "bar" and nodded.

We ordered cocktails and I followed Carmen to the back of the bar, up a staircase, and out onto a terrace strung up with fairy lights. It was still packed with people, but it was a relief to take my mask off and breathe in the fresh air. Carmen led me to a couple of stools by the railing.

"Imagine we were a couple though," I continued.

"Oh, this again," Carmen said, giggling.

"What would that look like?"

"Well, we would live wherever I'm based with the airline. At the moment that's Houston, which is also my hometown. It's convenient for me because my parents live there. And my *abuelita*. But that might not work for you. You would be an ocean away from your family."

"That sounds like a good thing."

Carmen frowned, stirring her Pina Colada.

"You don't get on with your family?"

"Nah, they're alright. I just don't need to see them that often."

"My family are everything to me. I literally cry when I can't see them."

"That's sweet," I said. It wasn't a lie, either. I couldn't imagine ever doing the same, and I felt a pang of shame at the thought.

"Don't you love your parents?"

"Of course," I answered. *Of course.* But my response was insufficient. And she knew it too, because she sat there and waited for me to continue. "I *do* love them. I just...find it difficult to be around them sometimes."

"Why?"

"I dunno," I said. "They're loving, helpful, and completely selfless. But sometimes I feel like I need to be away from them in order to become my own person. That's why I moved to London."

Carmen nodded slowly, taking another sip of her Pina Colada. I braced myself for some kind of counterargument, for her to tell me it was all in my head, but nothing came.

"I feel like I am who I am because of my family," Carmen said. "I'm just like my *abuelita*."

"Your what?"

"My nana," Carmen said.

"Oh."

"It makes me happy that I'm growing into her," she said. "So that's something you would have to get used to, if we were a couple."

"I would look after your nana while you're out of town," I said.

"What a gentleman," Carmen replied in a flat voice. Her sarcastic lips twisted into an amused smile. "What else would you do while I'm at work?"

"Well," I said, leaning forward. "I would obviously make sure the house is clean for when you get back. I think it would be depressing to fly around the world and come back to a messy house. So I'd always give it a proper clean the night before you come home."

"Thank you, I appreciate that."

"I figure you're probably tired after your shifts, so I would have wine ready for when you walk through the door. Sometimes I'd make a little charcuterie board for you. I'd give you a foot-rub while we watch some kind of soothing nature documentary."

"Attenborough?"

"Obviously."

Carmen finished her drink, leaning her elbow on the railing and twirling her hair around her finger.

"Keep going."

"We would have a sausage dog with floppy ears. That way I wouldn't feel alone when you're out of town for several days. Whenever you came back, he'd go crazy. Every time you walked through the door, you'd think it was your birthday. The dog would get so excited that it would take ages to calm him down. You would get set up on the couch and the dog would lay on your lap, savoring every second. I would pour the wine, and we would joke about how scared the dog probably was that one day you'd fly off and not come back."

Carmen gave me a relaxed smile.

"What's his name?"

"Nimrud."

She burst out in laughter then. It was a beautiful sound. We ordered more drinks and she asked me to describe the house. I'd never been to America, but I had an idea of what their big, suburban houses looked like from watching movies and TV shows. I imagined a place flooded with natural light. A front porch. A sleepy neighborhood of wide streets lined with trees.

I probably could have kept going all night, but Carmen suggested we check out another bar closer to Trafalgar Square. She told me I had a very active imagination and we left.

Out on the street, I asked her if her nana was worried about her working during the pandemic and she paused.

"She…" Carmen began, then cleared her throat. "So, my nana has dementia…"

"Shit, I'm sorry."

"It started to get worse right around the time the pandemic started, and now she hardly recognizes me."

Her face grew dark, and it looked like her eyes were glassy. We were getting close to the line outside the next bar.

"I used to visit her all the time before the pandemic. So even though I knew it would probably happen, I didn't expect her to forget me so quick. She just seems muddled, like she remembers some things but not others. I haven't been able to see her because she's old and my job means I'd put her at risk. It makes me so sad, because I can't help but feel that she probably misses me but can't remember exactly what she's missing. Like, she probably just feels this hole in her life without realizing what it is."

We came to a stop at the back of the line. In front of us a rowdy group of guys were laughing hysterically at something. Carmen sniffed. I rested my hand on her lower back, rubbing up and down gently. The line moved at a slow pace, and we were silent the whole time. We listened to the guys in front, who were oversharing without a trace of self-consciousness. I was curious what Carmen would make of them- how they might compare to guys from Texas- but I suspected she was only half-listening. By the time we made it to the bouncers, she had gotten her smile back.

Inside, the place rocked with dub and synth-pop. Not a mask in sight. *Fuck it*, I thought. The only place I wanted to be was right here. I didn't care what happened after Carmen left.

"I wanna go dancing!" Carmen yelled into my ear. She pointed beyond the bar, at the dance floor. I nodded, anxious not to lose her. The place was darker and more crowded than the last. The front room operated as a bar area, and either side of the long counter little steps led toward where the place turned into a club.

"Drinks?" I said, miming the action with my thumb and pinkie finger.

Carmen danced her way through the crowd to the end of the bar, tossing her hair and smiling at everyone she passed. She ordered us shots of tequila, which she downed with ease but which I struggled with. It had been a long time since I'd drank spirits, not that I'd ever done well with tequila. If I could, I avoided the stuff. But Carmen kept ordering it for us and I was determined to look onboard with her idea of fun.

At this point I wanted to keep a hold of her as long as possible. I kept thinking about how our goodbye would go, and how I could delay that moment. If I lost sight of her on the dance floor, there might not be a goodbye. It would be an unsatisfying way to end the day, to see her disappear into a mass of bodies. I imagined myself looking for her, finding nothing, and eventually trotting home in silence. It could happen. A dance floor could make us strangers again. She would lose herself in the joy of dancing, and only afterward she would remember our day together. I imagined she would look back on it fondly, probably not seeing anything unsatisfying about the way it ended. She was close to her hotel, she could dance as long as she liked, and it was obvious she wasn't tired yet. After all, I thought, she had no obligations to leave when I was tired. There were no rules about this date and how it might end.

You lost people all the time in clubs like that. Only usually, you would see them at work the next day and laugh about it. By the time I woke up tomorrow, Carmen would probably be in the air already.

Carmen knocked back her third shot of tequila and made for the dance floor. I grabbed her arm, pointing at the little booth where you could hand in your stuff for safekeeping. Carmen still had her handbag, and I still had my book on the Assyrian Empire. She laughed and shoved the book inside her handbag. It poked out but it just about fit inside.

It was surreal how unchanged the dance floor was from the pandemic. Everything was the way I remembered it. My last night out was New Year's Eve 2019, but that felt like it had happened years ago. As we squeezed through the crowd in search for a space to dance, I thought about how you wouldn't know there was a global pandemic going on from being in here. Not from the maskless faces. Not from Carmen, the way she danced. She pumped her chest and writhed her hips, running her hands up and down her sides. She looked like she was ecstatic to be alive. It was infectious. Her sheer excitement, her self-confidence. There was no way I would be able to keep up with her, but I was determined to stay as long as I could.

We tangled and untangled in the dark, together one minute and separate the next. Sometimes it felt like Carmen was dancing with me and other times it felt like she was dancing with everyone. I couldn't remember the last time I'd felt so invested in the present. All sense of time was lost—and I had no desire for it to come back. I wanted to nourish myself on her energy until it expired.

Each time we came together, Carmen got closer, her touch lingering on my body longer. My hands were on her waist, and she was grinding against me harder and harder. She leaned backward against my chest, as though trying to make eye-contact upside-down. She was still laughing her ass off. Then, just as it seemed we couldn't get any closer, she detached herself. Arms in the air, she bounced in circles on the balls of her feet, wholly independent once again. Then she was gone. A group of guys tumbled into the vacant space, as though the mass of dancers constantly adjusted itself to make sure that no square foot of floor was left unoccupied. It would be difficult to break through them. I paused for a moment and caught my breath.

I could get it over with and leave her to it. No matter how much I delayed things, the result would be the same. The next day she would fly back to America, and I would return to the monotony of furlough. It felt like the logical thing to do. Get an Uber back to Wimbledon while I still could and accept that our lives had already overlapped for as long as was possible. She wasn't mine and she never could be, so it made no sense to worry about what she did.

I was frozen like this for a while. If I stuck around, there was a chance we might dance again. Even though I knew it wouldn't affect how things ended, I couldn't leave while the possibility remained. *Just one more time*, I thought. *Just once.*

Slowly, I started to shuffle through the dance floor. Where there were no gaps, I made them, angling my shoulders sideways and carefully redirecting any bodies that came my way. The noise was deafening. Just then I felt old. When I was at university, I'd had this kind of stamina. I could go all night, right up until the clubs closed. I'd done it consecutive nights too. But now, just five years later, I didn't have it in me anymore. Just watching all those people bouncing up and down sapped my energy. I didn't belong here. *Fuck the book*, I thought. I'd just order it online. Right now, I had to get out.

I turned toward the exit and Carmen fell into my arms, laughing uncontrollably. Her arms were looped around my neck, and I held her around the waist. She looked up at me and asked something- something hilarious apparently. I blinked at her stupidly. I opened my mouth to ask what she meant but before I could speak, she pulled me down and kissed me. It was a sloppy, awkward kind of kiss, her tongue forcing my lips open for a brief second before she continued in a trail across my mouth and onto my chin. Hot tequila-breath poured into the back of my throat. She was on her tiptoes, pulling herself up against me as hard as she could.

We looked at each other for a brief moment and kissed again, this time slower, more coordinated. The next thing I knew we were getting her handbag back from the booth at the entrance. The whole time her hand never left mine. Then we were out on the street, the night air cooling the sweat on our necks. Just as suddenly, we were stumbling up the stairs of her hotel. She fumbled for the keycard to her room in her handbag. Next, she was pinning me to her bed, giggling as she held down my wrists, laying her weight flat upon me. Her kisses grew longer, the hot tequila-breath following her tongue as it slid down into my mouth. Carmen unbuttoned my shirt and I sat up. She remained in my lap, straddling me as she lifted my shirt off my shoulders and threw it on the floor. I pulled off her camisole and did the same thing.

After a while the giggling subsided, and she started to make tiny whimpering noises between each kiss. The only items of clothing that remained were my boxers and her panties. I rolled her over, wetting my fingers with my lips and touching her between her legs. For a while she kept making a sound as though she were gasping for air, placing her hand on top of mine as I rubbed her over the thin fabric. But then she grabbed my wrist and pulled my hand away. I asked if she wanted me to stop.

"No…" she panted. Since she was out of breath, her tone was ambiguous. I waited, and she said, "I want you to fuck me."

"Wait," I said. "I'll grab a condom."

"It's okay…I'm on the pill…"

"Wait," I said again.

All of a sudden, we felt like two naked strangers, our present situation inexplicable. It was like we had skipped a load of important steps and found ourselves at an intimacy we weren't equipped to deal with. That easy laughter of hers felt like a distant memory. We removed our underwear in silence. As I applied the condom, we avoided eye contact. I was conscious of Carmen masturbating as she waited for me, and my fingers trembled. The only sound in the room was her breathing. I finally secured the condom and got into position. As I parted her legs, my hands felt uncertain on her body, hesitant.

I entered her slowly and her entire body shuddered. Hands fastened themselves around my arms. I was conscious of the contours of her body, the warm, squishy press of her thighs. The involuntary noises she made that seemed to come from somewhere deep inside of her.

Within a minute, I had to pull out.

"Shit," I exclaimed. "I'm sorry."

Carmen collapsed onto the bed and let out a deep breath. "It's okay," she panted.

I made to touch her again between her legs, but she stopped me.

"You don't have to."

"I don't mind."

"It's okay," she said again.

We lay there panting for a while, our bodies distinctly separate. Eventually Carmen got up and went into the bathroom, closing the door behind her. I felt empty. I lay staring at the ceiling until I heard the bathroom door click open. A stranger came out.

"Hey, so I have to be up kinda early tomorrow…" she said.

"I'll get a cab."

I started to get dressed. The stranger stood there, holding an arm across her breasts. Total silence hung over the room.

Once I had my shoes back on, I opened Uber and selected my address. The little bar came up, searching for drivers. It was late but I would find one.

"I can wait downstairs," I said when the silence got to be too much.

She handed me my book in a way that seemed depressingly formal, neither of us looking at each other.

"Cheers," I said. She didn't walk me to the door. I pulled down on the handle, turned back, and said "See ya."

"Goodnight," she said in a small voice.

Out in the corridor, I gave a long exhale, rubbing my face. Then I looked up. I wasn't alone. A few doors down from where I was standing there was a woman. It only took me a second to remember her. It was the woman who had spilt her coffee on me earlier. A lifetime ago. We shared a blank look before she slotted her keycard into her door and I turned away, heading for the stairwell.

In the cab on the way home, I opened up Instagram and typed in the name *Carmen Solano*. Her profile appeared at the top of the suggested list. It seemed like she had posted regularly before the pandemic. I scrolled down to a photo from October last year, in Rio de Janeiro. She was wearing a sleeveless jumpsuit, hair in a high bun, hands in pockets. That same deadpan expression, as though she were waiting for you to impress her.

The caption read "Catch flights, not feelings" and below dozens of accounts had commented with fire emojis.

I clicked onto the tab that displayed the photos she had been tagged in. Her riding a mechanical bull, laughing at someone off-camera. Her sitting in an inflatable pineapple in an outdoor pool. Her shotgunning beer at a tailgate party.

My attention focused on a group photo, tagged at a Top Golf venue in Houston. There were six of them grinning at the camera. She was sat in the lap of some guy who had his arms around her midsection. Just like her, his arms had full tattoo sleeves. His face had a jagged, unfriendly shape. A strong jaw covered in a stubble beard that joined seamlessly with his buzzcut. I clicked on his profile, but it was private.

I closed out of the app and turned off my phone. Harry had sent me a message asking me how my day had gone. I knew that if I told him, he would act like it was wildly successful. And yet I felt depressed. Depressed to the point that I wondered if the whole thing had been worth it. But I couldn't articulate that to Harry. There was no way to make him understand. I knew logically that there was no possibility of her company extending any further than it had, and yet I felt incapable of simply being happy for the fun we had together. Harry would tell me to be happy and it would make complete sense. All I could think about was our lives getting ever more separate.

I knew that I would keep checking her Instagram periodically. I knew that I would feel rooted helplessly to the earth, thinking about all the places she went. I knew that there was no chance whatsoever that she would be thinking of me.

I knew that I was a fool.

The Layover III

The alarm shocked me from a dreamless sleep. After I switched it off, it took me a while to piece my waking life back together. I lay on my front, my mouth dry, feeling a pounding in my temple as though the alarm continued to echo there.

There was no trace of him anywhere in the room, just the clothes he had pulled off of me, strewn about the floor. My eyes rested on the black lace camisole in its tiny heap by the far wall. Less than 24 hours earlier I had been trying it on in the bathroom mirror, my brow furrowing at my figure. The cami still fit, but I'd put on a few pounds during the pandemic. I took a deep breath and held it, examining the look from various angles before exhaling. It had been two years since I'd fretted over an outfit like that.

And then, later that same day, he had lifted the camisole off of me as I straddled him. I recalled the hungry press of his hands on my tits, the clumsy pull of his lips on my nipples. My body ached for a new, unknown set of hands.

A stranger's lips. In that moment I felt new and exciting and mysterious for the first time in a long time. The way he looked at me, the way he touched me, made me feel somehow more real. Throughout the pandemic I had been floating, translucent, inconsequential. All of a sudden, I was grounded into the real world again. I was solid. I had weight. I was seen.

After he left, I'd put on my pajamas and chugged a glass of water. Even though it was late, I sat in bed for a long time. I thought about the date. He wasn't shy by British standards, but definitely shyer than the American men I'd been with. I'd figured out earlier in the evening that I would have to initiate to make anything happen. In the beginning he had pushed my buttons about Trump, COVID-19, and BLM until I realized he was just a devil's advocate. He didn't actually give a shit about any of it. For a while I thought he didn't give a shit about anything at all, but later that evening he revealed himself to be a kind of hopeless dreamer. His curiosity was endearing. He had let slip a restlessness, a playfulness too. I liked his low, gentle voice and his boxy physique. Most of all I liked his capacity for silliness. He took himself less seriously than most American men. It was an underrated quality. And so, I'd made the decision.

My second alarm shook me from the recollection, and I swiped it away with a groan. Within an hour I was showered, packed, and in my uniform. I met the other flight attendants in the lobby. Standing off to the side was Kelsey, dressed in the older uniform with the buttoned front. She had been furloughed much longer than I had during the summer. I instinctively made to avoid her, but then I felt bad and changed direction. As I approached, she turned toward me with a weak smile which I returned. It was a face that still felt so familiar. A face that had driven me mad at times. I reminded myself that she was a good person.

"Hey," I said.

"Hey."

"Um, I think I found something of yours," I said, and her eyebrows jumped. I reached into my handbag and removed a card with a professional photograph of two caramel-colored pugs snuggling in a laundry basket. Kelsey gaped.

"Holy shit, where did you find it?"

"That burger restaurant at the end of the street. I went there last night and noticed something had fallen down the crack of the seat. When I saw it, I recognized it immediately."

Kelsey took the card and let out a crazed, stunted laugh.

"We must have sat in the *exact* same booth."

"Lucky for you. How did you lose it? I thought you kept this in your purse."

"I've been using it as a bookmark," Kelsey said, gazing at the card in a way that told me she hadn't even realized she had lost it. "I was reading while I waited for my food. I guess it must have slipped out."

I shook my head slowly at her and giggled.

"Still the same Kels."

"*God*, I'm such a ding-dong."

Before we left the hotel, I asked her if she had any ibuprofen.

"Such a party girl," she said, handing me a box.

"Hardly."

"Sure seems like you had a good lay. I mean layover," Kelsey said, grinning at me like she knew something. I ignored her and swallowed the pill. The two of us had definitely had some crazy times together before the pandemic. Layovers in 13 different countries and almost every U.S. state. And plenty of adventures living together in Houston. Nothing was ever quiet with Kelsey. I smiled at her in thanks for the painkillers. She seemed happy and that made me happy. Even during the times I couldn't stand her, I always wanted the best for her.

On the way to the airport, I nourished myself with an iced mocha. The headache was receding, but I still felt tired. Today was going to be a long day. We were flying to Houston, instead of back to Chicago. That was a ten-hour flight. I'd get home in time for one sleep before jetting off to Phoenix the next morning. Still, I was glad to be living a busy life. If there was one thing I hated, it was sitting still.

*

You hate how white and suburban you actually are.

I'd said those words to Kelsey last year. I glanced over at her checking the seats and luggage compartments for any forgotten belongings, imagining the sting of what I'd said. Shitfaced at the 2019 Houston Pride Festival. Kelsey was the only white person there, but predictably she had dominated the conversation. Afterwards, our friend Terrell had taken me to one side.

What's the matter with you?

She's such a phony.

C'mon, Carm. You guys are best friends. Where's all this coming from?

I'd been a bitch that night. A whole year had passed, and I still didn't know what had set me off. My outburst had left her completely paralyzed. I wasn't known for yelling at people or losing my temper. When I encountered MAGA bigots, my tendency was to shut down and retreat into myself. And yet here I was, railing at someone whose views I was in complete alignment with. It was the first time I'd given Kelsey any cause to question our friendship.

Before that night, I'd suppressed the strange resentment that welled up inside me every time Kelsey posted about social issues on her Instagram. Every one of the posts she shared to her story I agreed with wholeheartedly. And yet a rage I didn't know I was capable of erupted, exclusively, at her.

You're Kelsey and Carmen, remember?

We finished our last checks and filled out the Cabin Checks Logbook. The plane was terminating here at Bush, so the captain turned off the power and we proceeded through customs. I caught up with Kelsey at the arrival gate. It dawned on me then that unlike me, she was no longer based here.

"Hey," I said. Kelsey was in the middle of a tigerish yawn. "Where are you staying?"

"Downtown at the Hyatt Regency. Then I'm doing Denver tomorrow. Then back to O'Hare."

"Wanna ride?"

Kelsey paused.

"I can get an Uber, it's fine."

"No, really. Nate is picking me up. It's not that far out of the way. Saves you the money."

"You sure?"

"Of course," I said, smiling at her. We fell into step beside each other and exited the terminal. Stepping outside for the first time after landing in Houston was always the same. That wave of dense, heavy air that washed over you. Kelsey used to say that it felt like swimming when you walked through it.

Nate's car pulled up and we put on our masks. I'd already told Kelsey about his Long Covid. We shoved our suitcases in the trunk and I opened the passenger door. To my surprise, Nate wasn't wearing his mask.

"Hey, is it okay if we give Kels a ride to her hotel?"

"Sure," he said. Even though it was late afternoon, he looked like he had just woken up.

Kelsey slid into the back and we set off.

"Hey, long time no see!" she exclaimed, a complete mismatch in energy levels.

"Hey," Nate said, barely making any effort.

"Thanks for the ride. Are you sure this is okay?"

"Yeah," Nate said.

I looked sideways at him. When we were together, I used to look forward to the times he was able to pick me up from the airport. There were usually tacos waiting for me on the dashboard. I kept my mask on, wondering if I should ask him where his was. I didn't feel like it was my place to nag him anymore, but the last time I'd come home from international duty, I'd given him the worst sickness of his adult life.

It was hard not to wonder if that had something to do with the way things ended between us. Maybe it had just expedited something that was already in motion.

"I'm staying at the Hyatt Regency."

Nate just nodded.

I was glad now that I had offered Kelsey the ride. It would have been a long drive back to the apartment without her. Nate turned south onto I-69, passing the gleaming car dealerships, the strip malls of baked concrete, and the short, dark-green hardwoods of coastal Texas. Lining the road toward the city were several billboards for local titty bars that

Kelsey used to find amusing. The downtown skyscrapers came into view in front of us like an island, surrounded in every direction by a flat, sprawling city. Having all the skyscrapers in one cluster like that meant you could see the nucleus of the city no matter where you were in it.

A year ago, the three of us had taken countless car journeys together. But now this arrangement felt different. I thought about all the times we had shared a car, from the apartment I had with Kelsey to a myriad of places across the city. Brunches of smoked salmon bagels in Montrose. Impromptu photoshoots at Buffalo Bayou or Discovery Green. Chill weekends at the aquarium, at top golf, at the Kemah Boardwalk. Beach days and pool days. What felt like a million midnight dashes to every kind of drive-thru the city had to offer. July 4th at Minute Maid.

You drove everywhere in Houston. It felt like the opposite of London. You couldn't just wander on foot to the local store, or just because you felt like wandering. Even the slightest errand here was a trip. Stranger still, the part of Houston that Kelsey and I had lived in was Upper Kirby- often abbreviated to U.K.- which was dotted with replicas of the red London phone booths. After our first international layover, we had asked Nate to take a photo of us with one of the replicas to match a photo Kelsey and I had taken of us with a booth in London. That was when Nate and I were just old school friends that slept together from time to time.

The idea of the three of us slipping back into who we were felt impossible now. Kelsey rambled about how much she preferred Europe to America in a stop-start kind of way, before eventually submitting to Nate's silence. When we dropped her off at her hotel she thanked us effusively, saying she hoped we would all get to hang out together soon. Nate and I smiled back, and I knew that it wouldn't happen. She waved one last time and disappeared inside the hotel, to a life that no longer overlapped with either of our own.

I kept thinking about Kelsey until I noticed that Nate was driving south, getting onto I-45.

"Where are we going?"

Nate sighed. His face had a pained expression.

"*Nate*. What is it? What's wrong?"

"I'm sorry," Nate managed, unable to look at me. "But while you were in London, your nana passed away."

"*What?*" I choked. The word started out as a scream but ended as a strangled whisper. I could feel all of the air rushing out of my body. It was difficult to breathe. My windpipe seemed to contract and my breathing became ragged. Almost instantly, as though they had been lying in wait, hot tears filled my eyes.

"I'm sorry," Nate said, his face pale and sleepless. Bloodshot eyes focusing on the traffic. "But it's true."

"When?"

"Yesterday afternoon."

I blinked, cracking the film of tears that blocked my vision and sending them pouring down my cheeks. I took my glasses off and buried my face in my hands, unable to stop myself from sobbing. The sobs rocked my body and shattered the silence of the car. I couldn't help it.

"I'm sorry," Nate said for a third time.

Everything was a blur until we reached Friendswood. I felt Nate turn off of the interstate, into our old neighborhood, and tried to wipe the tears from my face.

"How?"

"They said she didn't feel nothing."

"Was it Covid?"

"I don't know. I don't think so."

I felt dizzy. I must have looked it too, because Nate told me to focus on breathing. The old neighborhood blurred past me, leafy and familiar. This was where me, my parents and my nana had first settled in America. Where I had gone to school with Nate and pelted him with water balloons in the summers. And where my father had chosen to buy his mother a house of her own when he had saved up the money.

Nate parked on the street outside Nana's house and I noticed my parents' Silverado in the driveway. I put my glasses back on with shaking hands, hearing Nate shut the door behind him. A moment later he opened the door on my side and asked if I felt faint.

"I'm fine," I said, unbuckling my seatbelt. He continued to stand close to me as we walked up the driveway. I wasn't aware of putting one foot in front of the other, of the solid ground that met each step. I floated up toward the front door and opened it.

I found my two parents in the living room, looking as though they hadn't uttered a sound in hours. My father was sat in an armchair and I went to him, pulling my mask down to my chin and collapsing at his feet. I buried my face in his knee and the sobbing started up again. My father held onto me, leaning forward to stroke my back with his left hand and my head with his right. He didn't try to say anything. Just the sight of him as I entered the room had broken me.

Papa was not a man that cried. In fact, I don't remember him crying about anything, ever. But sat in that armchair, a single, silent tear descended the left side of his face. In contrast, my mom- whom I had seen cry often- was the one holding it together. I heard her get up from the couch to kiss Nate out of instinct before apologizing for breaking Covid-etiquette.

"Don't worry about it," Nate said.

"Thank you for getting her here safely," she said.

Then I was aware of her kneeling down beside me on the floor, of her hugging me from the other side. Nothing about any of this was how I'd imagined it. Nothing except this- my parents and I all holding onto each other. I continued to wail, and my parents continued to caress me until I eventually fell silent.

"I'll make some coffee," Nate said. "Y'all take a moment."

I heard his footsteps fading in the direction of the kitchen.

"Papa," I whimpered at last, lifting my head from his lap and looking at him. I reached out and wiped the solitary tear from his cheek. He gazed back at me with soft eyes. I always said that my father had soft eyes in a hard face. It was a strong, square-shaped face and his eyes were small and dark. "I'm sorry."

"She was a saint," Mom said, and I felt her left hand leave my shoulder. I knew it was tracing the sign of the cross over her chest. Her right hand rubbed my lower back.

"Who…how…"

"I found her yesterday. She wasn't answering her phone."

"Why…"

"You were in Europe," Mom said. Her voice was strong and sure of itself. "There was no upside to telling you before you got home."

"I'm so sorry," I said to Papa. It seemed very difficult for him to speak, but his eyes never left mine.

My glasses were on the end of my nose and Mom removed them for me, placing them on the coffee table.

"Come on," she said in a light voice. "Come sit down, Carmen."

I kissed my father's hands and took a seat on the couch, trying to catch my breath. Mom sat next to me, her arm around my shoulders. After a while, Nate came back in the room and served us coffee.

"Thanks, son," my father said. His choice of words struck me. While Nate knew my parents well enough, they weren't especially close or anything. We had dated for a year before moving in together, during which he had started to see them more, but then the pandemic happened. Nate placed a creamy coffee next to me and I knew that he had taken the time to make it exactly how I liked it.

I drank, thinking how long the day had been. My body was still operating on British time, so it felt like 10pm. And I hadn't gotten much sleep on account of the night before. My memory stretched back to where the day began in my London hotel room, which somehow felt both near and far.

"Have you eaten, Carmen?" Mom said.

I shook my head, chugging the last of the coffee and placing the cup back on the table with trembling fingers. I wiped my mouth on the sleeve of my creased blouse.

"You should eat something."

"I can't."

My eyes focused then on the armchair opposite the one my father was in. My *abuelita's* chair. No one had ever dared sit in it when she was alive, and they didn't dare now. It had the best angle of the TV and was adorned with plush toys I had gifted her down the years. I wondered then if that was where my mom had found her. It was as likely a place as any.

My eyes strained as they scanned the chair for evidence of her body's recent imprint.

Seeing what I was looking at, Papa said gently, "She loved you so much."

"So much, Carmen," Mom said, caressing my back. I started crying again, unable to look at it any longer, but I didn't sob this time. I just cried silently in the silent room.

As long as I could remember, Nana had never been far away. Not until the pandemic. She had lived close to us in Costa Rica, had lived with us for our first few years in the United States, and had lived a few blocks away after that. I had always had access to her whenever I wanted it. Her place at the dining room table felt as immutable as the oak it was made out of.

But then she had started to forget things. Items, appointments, names. And then the pandemic happened. I had assumed that when it was all over, everything would resume as normal, and I would be over here at her house all the time. The idea that she- of all people- would leave me as a stranger, was unthinkable.

We sat for a long time in her living room, sometimes talking, but most of the time just sitting there in silence. The funeral was going to be at the end of the week. Mom was taking care of it. Our family back in Costa Rica all wanted to come but Mom thought it was a bad idea. Papa said nothing. It was going to be a quiet funeral. I could see it- just the three of us sitting in an otherwise empty church. The rest of the family on Zoom.

"It's getting late," Mom said at last, rising from the couch. Papa sighed and followed suit, scratching his chin. Another thing about my father was that he always had the presence of a man taller than he actually was. It was in the way he carried himself. Even though he had long ago been promoted to supervisor, he still had a machinist's body.

But as my mom placed a hand on his shoulder and guided him toward the door, he suddenly looked small for the first time.

"You should get some rest," Mom said, turning back to look at us.

"I want to stay here for a while," I said.

"Make sure she eats something," Mom said to Nate. He nodded and they left.

Sometime after we heard them pull out of the driveway, I told Nate that he didn't have to stay. He had already done more than enough. But he just shrugged and said, "It's alright."

*

I fell asleep on Nana's bed upstairs, hoping she would come to me in my dreams. When Nate gently shook me awake, I didn't know where I was. My fingers clutched at the dark greens, browns, blues, and burgundies of the bedsheet's floral pattern. The night before last, she had slept here. I wondered if dementia affected dreams or not. Perhaps I had lingered there, whenever she laid her head here at night. I imagined my own face disappearing in the mornings, and her, confused, feeling that the dream had been real.

"I ordered some pizza," Nate said presently.

"I'm not hungry."

"You should eat."

Downstairs, we ate in silence at the small kitchen table. The light above us was the only light on in the entire house. By now it was dark outside. Two pizzas- one pepperoni and one Hawaiian- lay in their boxes, and we ate them out of their boxes. It turned out I was hungrier than I'd felt. For his part, Nate ate sheepishly, saying nothing.

We had finished about half of each pizza when we stopped.

"Here," Nate said, handing me a coke.

I took a long draw from the coke, drinking half the can before wiping my nose on my sleeve and looking up at him.

"Thank you," I said. "You didn't have to stay."

"S'alright."

"You still don't."

"I can leave...do you want that?"

"I don't know," I said. I looked back at the pizzas, unable to eat anything more. Nate must have had a small appetite too, and after a while he combined the leftovers into one of the boxes and placed it in Nana's fridge. We drank our cokes and I gazed around the kitchen. It seemed as though remnants of her were everywhere. The chipped wood of the table's edge; a table that had always seemed old, even when it was new. My father had scolded me for picking at it one time. It seemed always to be flaking away, forever peeling. I figured there would always be more. That, just like Nana, it would never actually give out.

I ran my thumb along it, taking pleasure in its tiny crevices.

"I want to sleep here tonight, in Nana's bed," I said.

Nate just nodded.

"You can go home if you want."

"I'll take the couch," he said.

I wasn't tired, even though I ought to be. Nate sat there for a while longer before getting up and looking through Nana's pantry. I continued to finger the edge of the table. It was strange to be sitting here after so long. Strange to be sitting here without her. Before the pandemic I always came over with the intention to do something useful for her- to cook for her, to do the dishes, to tidy up. But Nana always kept her house in order so well that I'd end up sat here, at this table, while she fussed over me. No matter how hard I tried to reverse the dynamic of my childhood, it remained the same, and I would ultimately submit to the way she tended to me. As long as she was alive, I would always be the little girl picking at the chipped table while she fixed me an iced tea and told me stories about the village she had grown up in.

To me it was a mythical place. As vividly as she brought it to life, I couldn't imagine my Nana as a little girl. I could barely wrap my head around the idea that she had had a whole life of her own before I was born. When she talked about that village- deep in the colorful interior of the country, far from San José, where I was born- it felt like she must have been talking about someone else's life. The girl that ran barefoot down the jungle road to tell her father and uncles about approaching cars of tourists couldn't be the same one that had sat here in this kitchen, complaining about telemarketing scams, watching the Astros game, and eating Blue Bell ice cream.

Nate was making me a chamomile tea. He hadn't asked me if I wanted it, which was just like Nana. He placed it before me and I thought back to when he had Covid- the Covid I'd given him from one of my international flights. He had twisted and turned on that couch for a month, his whole body racked with aches and burning up a fever. But I had nursed him, just as he nursed me now.

My thumb caught in one of the little fissures of the wooden table and I picked at it. A white flake of painted wood tumbled to the floor. Right up until the end, Nana hadn't let me reverse the roles and take care of her. Perhaps I should have left the airline when the pandemic hit. That way I could have checked in on her when she needed me the most.

As I stared at the white flake, Nate mumbled something about getting ready for bed. But I was a million miles away. I was in this kitchen, a dozen years ago, with her tending to me.

As a teenager I went through a phase of running away from home and ending up here.

I can't go back. Papa is going to kill me.

He won't.

Whenever my father came to pick me up, he never said anything. I would be sat in this same chair, listening to his heavy footsteps coming up the hallway and reaching a stop behind me. Nana would look at me from the other side of the table and say it.

It's time to go home now, Carmen.

The car ride home was silent too. My father drove with a stunted, impotent twist to his square face- and I knew that Nana's protection would last for a while yet.

At fifteen I turned up shitfaced on her porch. I didn't ring the bell because it was past midnight already, but Nana was still up and the porch light gave me away. She held my hair as I puked into the toilet, and she continued to hold me afterwards when I sobbed.

I'm so dead...I'm so, so dead...I can't...He can't...

I didn't know what Papa would be angrier about- that I'd been drinking alcohol or that I'd been doing so with boys. Going back in that state was unthinkable. But Nana continued to caress my hair and told me I could stay.

I'd slept in her bed with her that night, with the guilty understanding that, regardless of how drunk I was, I'd known full well that she would take care of everything when I arrived. It was the same instinct that had guided me there when I used to run away.

Looking back on it now, I couldn't help but shudder. I'd exploited her that night to get out of facing my father. My brain seemed intent on punishing me by focusing on that memory ahead of all the others.

You won't tell him?

No, I won't tell him. But please be more careful, Carmen…

I physically shuddered. That was one debt I really wish I had repaid. Now it was too late.

*

The memory continued to punish me as I lay on Nana's bed. Through the wall I could hear Nate brushing his teeth, and I tried to focus on that sound. Eventually the sound of the running faucet stopped and there was silence. Then the flick of the light switch, followed by his footsteps on the landing, heading for the stairs.

"Nate," I called out. The door was open a crack and I heard the footsteps stop. "Can you come in here for a moment?"

A pause. After a few seconds, the footsteps came toward the door and he pushed it open enough to poke his head in.

"Yeah?"

I gazed at his silhouette. That long neck. I could make out the pointed shadow of his Adam's Apple.

"Come in," I said.

He came in and looked down at me in the dark.

"You're still wearing your uniform," he said.

"I know."

"Want me to grab your bag from the car?"

"No."

"What do you want?"

I took a breath. "Can you sleep in here tonight?"

The gangly silhouette went silent.

"I dunno."

"Please?"

"I can take the couch, it's fine."

"I don't want to be alone."

Nate sighed. He turned out the light in the upstairs hallway and closed the door to just a crack. It was pitch-dark and I was aware of him moving around to the other side of the bed. Just then there was a sudden crash near my feet.

"Christ!" Nate exclaimed and I burst out laughing. It was a silent, breathless laughter though, as though my sobbing earlier had used up all the residual air in my lungs. "Fucking Zimmer frame," he grunted, hobbling around the bed and sitting down. It wasn't until he lay down under the covers that he was aware I was laughing uncontrollably.

"What's gotten into you?" he said. I couldn't answer him, couldn't do anything except laugh soundlessly into the pillow. "Damn, you're in hysterics. Your mind's touched the void, Carm."

I didn't think I'd ever stop. I took long breaths but then it tumbled out of me again.

"Really?" he said.

"You're such a dildo."

"Thanks."

We lay there in silence on Nana's bed for a while. I couldn't tell if Nate had his eyes open.

"I was a shit granddaughter."

"No, you weren't," Nate said. "You were over here all the time."

"I should have been here for her during the pandemic."

"You couldn't."

"All I ever did was take from her."

"She wanted to give," Nate said. It was true. "Your company was all she wanted, and you gave her that. I barely used to see my grandparents when they were alive. I was selfish. I didn't visit them because it was boring and I didn't know what to say. Then they were gone. At least you did all you could."

"Not *all* I could."

"Enough though."

We were silent again. Minutes passed. I inched closer to him on the mattress but he didn't react. His body was completely still. I couldn't even detect his breathing. I inched closer once again, so that I could feel his breath on my face. Still he didn't say anything, didn't move a muscle. I waited for a minute, then I reached for him. My hand was probably cold on his stomach but he didn't react. I slid down and cupped the warm bulge in his boxer shorts.

"No," he said, shuffling out of reach. "We can't... I can't."

"Please..."

"No," he said, firmer this time. He sat up, breathing heavily. I couldn't make out his expression. He was perched on the edge of the bed, as far away from me as possible.

"I slept with someone, in London," I said. I don't know why I said it. There was total silence for a moment.

"That's none of my business," Nate said. "We ain't together anymore."

"Right," I said.

He got out of the bed.

"You're trying to provoke me because you feel like you deserve to be hated right now. Well, it ain't working."

"Just go," I said. "Just get out."

Nate sighed but didn't protest. He left the bedroom. I listened to his footsteps descend the staircase, then disappear as they must have met the living room carpet. The house was still for a minute before the footsteps reappeared in the downstairs hallway for a brief moment. The front door opened and then closed. The footsteps faded down the driveway. The car engine started, and then I heard him drive off down the road, into the night.

I clutched at the bedsheets, not finding my *abuelita* in their texture. They were just sheets, stiff and clean. Tears welled up in my eyes again, and I got out my phone. Without thinking about what I was doing, I called Kelsey. After the third ring I cancelled the call. A stupid idea. A minute later, she called back. I didn't answer it. A second passed and then she texted me.

Everything ok?

Sorry, misdial, I typed back.

Now, I realized, I was truly alone.

Unanswered Messages

I almost didn't stop when I saw him flagging me down on the highway with a bandana, twenty miles from town. His car had broken down, although I couldn't tell just from looking what was wrong with it. I was almost past him when I started breaking, and all I could think about as I stepped out of the car was that he must have noticed my hesitation. Dense rows of quaking aspen covered the bluffs either side of the road, and I figured we were probably the only two people around for miles. Maybe it was being a young woman traveling alone, maybe it was watching too many serial killer documentaries, or maybe it was just the craziness of that summer. The country seemed like a place where anything could happen at any moment.

The man looked to be in his fifties, wearing pale jeans and a soiled white tank. He had a beat, ruddy face, as though it had aged more rapidly than the rest of his body from being out in the sun too long. There was no cell reception up here, so he needed a lift into town.

"Appreciate it," he said when he got in the car. He had a thin gray moustache threaded with sweat.

"Would you mind putting a mask on?" I asked him, and I felt my insides contract. The man stared at me for what felt like a long time before letting out a single, dry chuckle.

"You serious?"

"I'd really appreciate it," I said. I offered him a smile, but he probably couldn't tell because I already had my own mask on.

"I ain't got one," he said in a tight voice.

I opened up the glove compartment and held one out to him. He paused, looking down at it as though I were asking him to degrade himself in some way. His brow furrowed and he bit the corner of his lip. I didn't know if he could tell or not, but I was shaking.

At that moment, my Bengal cat Greedo emitted a long, frustrated meow from his carrier in the back seat. I hadn't let him out in hours. He pressed his face into the netted divider and repeated the sound. The man glanced back at him, before seeming to sigh as he accepted the face mask in my hand.

"Thank you," I said again, desperate to show I was friendly.

We drove in silence for a while, the road zig-zagging down the mountainside under the shade of towering fir trees. The canopy made sparse puddles of the sun on the asphalt. I blinked, adjusting to the change in the light.

"You know, masks don't do anything," the man said. "It's all about control."

I decided not to reply. I gripped the steering wheel tighter and tried to focus on driving. The trees grew sparse and sunlight flooded my vision again, shooting through the gaps between the trunks. When the firs parted I got a glimpse of the small city in the valley below, cushioned on all sides by the Rocky Mountains.

"Just sayin'," the man said. "No offense or whatever."

He looked around at Greedo and all my belongings stacked around his carrier and in the trunk of the station wagon. Tupperware boxes of silverware that jangled now and then. Cardboard boxes of poetry books, hiking gear, and thrifted blouses. Black bags of towels and jackets and sheets and throws. Two dozen coat hangers that rattled together. I kept checking the rearview mirror to make sure everything was securely in place.

"You new in town, then?" he said.

"Yep."

"What do you do?"

"I'm a travel nurse," I said. "ICU."

"Ah..." the man said in an ambiguous tone. We were silent for a while and I hoped it would stay that way, but then he said, "I'm Jim by the way. What's your name, hun?"

I didn't want to tell him, but I figured I had no choice.

"Audrey."

"Where you from, Audrey?" he said. "Originally, I mean."

I knew what he was driving at. I took a quiet breath and answered in a stiff voice, "Seattle."

"Huh," Jim said. He sounded surprised. His mouth opened to say something else.

"My parents emigrated from Taiwan, but I was born here."

Jim made a "Hm," sound as if now I was talking sense, but he didn't comment on this information. He sniffed and fidgeted a lot when he wasn't talking. Now and then, I could feel him looking at me.

"Let me guess," he said after another pause. "As a nurse, you've probably seen some shit, right?"

"Yeah, you could say that."

"Covid?"

"Yeah, I've treated Covid patients."

"And I bet all of them were fine, except the ones who were going to die anyway, am I right?" he said. I didn't answer him. "I heard it has like a 99% percent survival rate."

"It's not the survival rate that makes it so bad. What makes it bad is how infectious it is."

"Still," Jim said. "I think everyone overreacted to it."

"Funny how so many living people say that," I said. Jim snorted and we didn't talk until we reached the city.

I asked him where I should drop him off and he said he would guide me.

"A buddy of mine runs an auto shop. Just take me to him."

My GPS was set to my new apartment, so when I turned left at Jim's direction, it started freaking out and trying to course-correct. As this was happening, I was super-conscious of the fact that my address was on the screen. Ten minutes later, we stopped outside the auto shop. Jim didn't get out.

"Thanks, Audrey. You're a real doll," he said.

"No problem."

"Why don't you come in for a beer? Kevin's got a cooler in the back. He'd get a real kick out of your opinions I bet."

"Sorry, but I have to get going," I said, and the contracting feeling returned to my torso.

"Come on. You must be tired after a trip like that. One beer."

"I have to go," I said, unable to look at him.

He was silent then and I wondered if he would ever get out. His gaze weighed heavily on my face and I could feel my cheeks burning.

"Alright, alright," he said, chuckling. "I'll see you around, hun."

Jim got out then and I loosed a breath I didn't know I'd been holding for so long. As soon as the door shut, I put the car in drive and followed the GPS back the way I came. In the rearview mirror, I could see him standing on the sidewalk, staring after me.

*

Exhausted, I stepped into the bar and found it mostly empty. It was late afternoon at this point and still bright outside. A young woman behind the bar looked at me and seemed to be smiling behind her mask, though it was hard to tell. I walked up to her.

"Audrey Tang?" she said.

"Yes," I panted, helping myself to some hand-sanitizer at the counter. "I'm here to see Mr. French."

"That's my dad," the woman said, placing a dishcloth over her shoulder. "He's out of town at the moment but he told me to help move you in. He'll be back tonight to meet you, or he can come over in the morning if you prefer. I'm Brenna by the way."

Brenna reached beneath the bar and produced a set of keys, handing them to me. Then she replaced the dishcloth and called for a guy in the kitchen to watch the bar for her.

"You must be tired," she said as we went out onto the street.

"Yep."

"Where are you driving from?"

"Phoenix."

"Damn. That's quite the road trip," Brenna said. "Well, welcome to Colorado."

I didn't have the stamina to be affable, so I just nodded. The apartment building was a short walk down the street. Brenna seemed chill with not talking. We arrived where I had parked my car outside the front entrance and I checked on Greedo before joining Brenna at the door. The apartment building was square-shaped with painted wood paneling and two floors. Brenna told me which key did what and pretty soon I was standing in an alcove studio on the first floor that looked out over the rear parking lot. The L-shaped room was mostly furnished, with the bedroom being divided not by a wall but what looked like a modern bookcase with cubed sections. I could fill the cubes with cacti and volumes of feminine rage, I thought to myself. A beaded curtain connected the bookcase to the wall. I didn't exactly need privacy from myself, but it was a nice touch.

Brenna pointed out a hook halfway down the wall to clip the beads to one side, but I said I liked the idea of walking through them. It would make the apartment feel more like two rooms than one, which is what it actually was. When she was done with the spiel, Brenna offered to help me move in my things. I said I was fine and she shrugged.

"You know where to find us if you need anything. Come by the bar later and I'll give you a cold one on the house."

I smiled and gave a non-committal answer. I spent the rest of the day unpacking, listening to acid jazz, and watching my cat. A few people walking down the street offered to help but I insisted I was fine. I didn't have too much. When everything was out of the car, I moved it around to the lot at the back of the building and ordered a pizza. Even though I'd been on the road for several days, I didn't feel like being around people. In the evening, I tied my fairy lights around the apartment and turned out all the other lights. Mr. French called and apologized for not being here when I arrived, but I said it was fine. I blinked sleepily at my new home and thought: *everything really is as fine as it needs to be.*

*

I had until Monday until I'd be back in scrubs, so I used the rest of the week to buy stuff for the apartment and walk around the neighborhood. A river snaked through the city and I crossed an old railroad bridge to find a thrift store on the other side. The woman at the counter gave me a list of cafes to try out downtown. Downtown was a long street of old brick buildings that reminded me of the Wild West. Everything was pedestrianized with streets and plazas of red bricks. Trees lined the main road and there were posters in shop windows advertising music festivals and a farmer's market.

I kept walking past the bar on my street but I didn't go back inside. I couldn't decide if it was a good thing to have my landlord so close or not. A normal person probably would have thought it was a good thing, but I'd grown accustomed to not letting people see too much of me.

On the Friday I reluctantly admitted this to my therapist. She said she thought it would be a good idea for me to try and make friends in my new city and I pouted, looking away from the laptop screen.

Dr. Kauffman cleared her throat and asked me if my father knew where I was living now. I sighed.

"Not yet. I like to enjoy a few weeks where no one knows where I am. It's very therapeutic for me."

"Yes, I remember you doing the same thing when you moved to Phoenix," Dr. Kauffman said. "I think it would be a good idea to call him though. Not just to let him know you're safe, but to catch up."

Dr. Kauffman was always advocating for at least a semi-functioning relationship with my father. He continued to pay for the therapy, even after all these years, but he never asked me about it. He didn't ask if it was helpful, or even if I was still going.

"It doesn't have to be every day," she said. "Maybe you can try to schedule one call a month."

"I'll think about it," I said in the voice I used to indicate I wanted to change the subject.

"One more thing," Dr. Kauffman said, "as we're running short on time. And I want you to be honest. Have you registered with a pharmacy there yet?"

"No."

"I think you should try and do that as soon as you can. Okay?"

I didn't say anything. I was watching Greedo enviously through the cubed bookcase as he stretched himself out on my bed.

"I don't want you to put it off and then only register when your prescription runs out. It's important to stay consistent with the medication during big changes in your life- such as moving to a new state."

"I know," I said. Dr. Kauffman had transitioned to her delicate voice.

"In the past you've left it too late and it's not been good for you. I know you've hinted many times about coming off

114

of the pills, but I want you to promise me that when you do come off, it's in a controlled manner and you consult me first. Don't come off of them on a whim. And definitely don't come off of them out of laziness. Just get the registration over with and reward yourself afterwards."

"Okay, I promise."

"See you next week, Audrey. Best of luck this Monday."

I signed off of the Teams Meeting and shut my laptop. For a while I lay back on the couch and closed my eyes. A nap was definitely on the cards, but I still had things to sort out that afternoon. Greedo's eyes cracked open and we stared at each other through the bookcase. It felt like a profound exchange.

When I checked my cell, I noticed I had a new friendship request on Facebook. My throat went dry when I read the name. Jim Groff. I clicked his profile and sure enough, it was the man I had given a ride to on the day I moved in. His profile picture had a banner of the American flag with the words "All Lives Matter" written across it in blocky yellow Sans Serif font. I didn't want to think about how he had tracked me down, or how long it had taken him to do so. My finger hovered over the screen for a moment, but in the end I neither accepted nor declined him.

When I checked my inbox, I saw that he'd tried to send me a message. I wasn't sure if it let the other person know that you'd viewed it if you weren't friends with them, but I opened the message anyway.

All it said was: *Hey Audrey it's Jim. Thanks again for the help the other day.*

I closed out of the app and started pacing around the apartment. The thought I couldn't shake was that this man had had my new address displayed in front of him for the whole drive. I'd mentioned this to Dr. Kauffman, and how I couldn't stop thinking about whether I should have stopped the car or not.

"I didn't have time to think it through. I went round a bend and there was this guy asking for help. In the end I panicked. It seemed like the right thing to do."

Dr. Kauffman didn't give me an answer one way or the other on whether it was a good decision, but she said she was proud of me for trying to help the man.

"I'm just so on edge these days," I'd said to her. "I never know if I'm overreacting or not."

"You've had a tough year, Audrey. We both know that."

*

That evening, I was going crazy in my apartment and decided to finally check out the bar. It did seem nice to have a place like that so close- I was just anxious about becoming too familiar. The city was beautiful at dusk. Every lighted window looked cozy and even in the dark, you were aware of the mountains insulating the city on all sides, as high as the stars.

The bar was a long, two-story brick building. A sign out front read "Frenchie's Saloon". Inside, the place was a lot more lively than it had been the day I arrived. The walls were lined with impressive taxidermy pieces, including a grizzly bear, an elk, and a moose. There were also non-American animals, such as a cape buffalo hanging above the entrance to the shitter. The walls also featured framed newspaper front pages that looked like they could be from anywhere between 1890 and 1930. Transparent plastic dividers had been erected between the tables and booths to help encourage social distancing. A sign at the entrance requested that you wear a mask whenever you weren't sat down.

The ceiling was very high, which I liked, and lined all the way down with fans. I took a seat on one of the barstools and waited for Brenna to notice me. She was wearing a tan flannel shirt that I thought suited the aesthetic of the place. As she poured a Coors Light for a man at the end of the bar, I admired the neon signs on the walls that juxtaposed with the framed sepia photos of miners.

"How's the cat settling in?" Brenna asked when she came over to me.

"Aren't you gonna ask about me first?"

"No. The cat's ok then?"

"He's swell. Little shit that he is. I'm also fine."

"Didn't ask," Brenna said, cocking her head at me. She had a husky, deadpan kind of voice that made me think of a hand-cranked ice-crusher. "So, what can I do you for?"

"I was wondering if I could still redeem that beer on the house you mentioned. I like free beer."

Brenna narrowed her eyes at me and slid over a menu. Then she went to serve someone else while I perused it. All of the items on the laminated sheet were craft beers. I couldn't decide what to choose so when Brenna came back, I ordered a Heineken. She frowned at me.

"You're going to use your free drink on something you can buy anywhere?"

I shrugged. "I know what I like."

"No, you don't," Brenna said. She poured me something from a tap I couldn't make out and I didn't protest. A moment later she presented me with a snifter glass filled with a dark pink ale. "Try this," she said.

"It's pink."

"This one's brewed with hibiscus leaves. Smell it."

I lowered my nose to the rim of the glass and felt the flowery fragrance coil its way up my nostrils. I made a little noise to convey that I was impressed. Brenna leaned on the bar with both hands and watched me until I'd taken a drink. For some reason I smacked my lips and exhaled expressively.

Brenna raised an eyebrow.

"It's good. Hibiscussy."

"You're weird."

Although I'd only intended to stay for just the one beer, I ended up staying there the whole night and ordering three more off the menu (which I dutifully paid for). Sitting at the bar conversing with another person felt somehow safer than being alone in my apartment. Between serving customers, Brenna would circle back to me to chew the fat. I liked to think that I was making her shift more fun, although she gave no indication one way or the other that she appreciated my company. I learned early on in the evening that Brenna was allergic to any kind of sincerity, which was something I respected.

Brenna lived in a studio above the bar that she rented from her dad for what was a token amount, which sounded like a pretty sweet deal to me. She worked full-time at the bar on opposite shifts to Mr. French and seemed, from what I could tell, quite content with her situation. I also learned that she had a major in music production and sound recording that she didn't use (and wasn't sure that she ever would). She asked me what brought me to Colorado.

"Murder hornets," I answered without skipping a beat. "Figured I'm safe up here in the mountains. That's the main reason. Also, I'm a travel nurse."

"Travel nurse?" Brenna said. "That's a thing?"

"Yep."

"So you just go from hospital to hospital?"

"Pretty much. I'm a tumbleweed."

"Doesn't that get lonely, constantly uprooting yourself?"

I shrugged.

"I just mean, like, having to leave your friends and make new ones all the time. I don't think I'd be able to do that. Do you know anyone here?"

"Just you."

"We've basically just met."

"I know. I've already marked you out as my best friend in Colorado. First, best, and only friend that is."

"I don't think I'm ready for that responsibility," Brenna said, taking my empty glass and cleaning it.

"Well, you're stuck with me now. I'll be over all the time."

Brenna made a face before drifting over to a waiting customer. The bar was closing soon and she hollered at the remaining patrons that she would now be taking last orders. I wondered why I was so unwilling to leave and then I remembered Jim's message.

I checked Facebook Messenger and refreshed the page. Since I had been at Frenchie's Saloon, Jim Groff had sent me another message- which told me that he was aware I'd seen his first one. This time it said: *How are you.* Even though he'd opted to forgo the question mark, I could feel my heart palpitating at the request for a direct response. I didn't even notice when Brenna came back over to me.

"Last orders," she said. I was still staring at my cell phone with my mouth hanging open. I sensed Brenna leaning over the bar on her forearms then. "Everything okay?" she said. Most of the customers had shuffled out of the door by this point. A few called goodnight to Brenna. Two drunk guys in a corner booth seemed to be debating whether to get one more round before the place closed up.

I told Brenna about the day I had moved in, from the moment Jim had flagged me down on the mountain road to the moment I dropped him off. When I showed her the conversation thread, she grimaced like I'd shown her stills of an open-heart surgery.

"I don't know," I said. "It's probably nothing."

"It's definitely sketchy."

I told her about my address being on the GPS screen and asked her if I was being paranoid.

"Wait here until I close up. I'll walk you home."

"You don't have to do that. It's only a five-minute walk."

"Girl, you've had four beers."

"I'm offended you think I can't handle my drink."

"Like you said, it's only a five-minute walk. It wouldn't be getting in my way."

Brenna wasn't the kinda chick to take no for an answer. When the last customers left the bar, a kitchen porter came out to mop up. He stacked the chairs on the tables and Brenna told him to watch the place for a few minutes.

When we were outside, I admitted I was in fact a little tipsy. It wasn't something I had even noticed coming on when I was sat down chatting. It manifested in awkward, uncertain footsteps on the sidewalk. I heard myself slurring my words and wondered how long this had been going on for.

"I told you. You're lit. I know the look."

"Thanks for walking me home."

"It's nothing. And if this guy ever gives you any trouble, send him my way. The shotgun under the bar usually does the trick."

"You have a shotgun under there?"

"It's a saloon, of course we do. It's practically the law," she said with a wry smile.

We were quiet for a moment as we reached the apartment building. No creepers in sight. I tried to stop thinking about it, as though being paranoid would somehow make it a likelier reality.

"You might not see me for a while," I said, stopping at the path to the front entrance. "I start work on Monday, which means I start isolating."

"Shit, I guess that makes sense."

"You've got a neat place back there, but I feel like I'd be putting everyone at risk if I came back."

"No, I get it," Brenna said, resting her hands in the back pockets of her jeans, thumbs out. There was a pause, in which the only noise was a distant police siren, before we wished each other goodnight.

*

On the Sunday, I decided to do a lot of things I knew I wouldn't have the energy for once I was back in the ICU. In the morning I put on a summer dress, aviators, and an olive fedora, stopping at the mirror to take strength from the look before heading out. I found a bench by the river and called my father.

"I live in Colorado now," I told him in English.

"Oh," he said. He asked me for my new address and I promised to send it to him. I asked him then how he had been and he didn't have much to say. During the call we seemed to say little of anything specific. He asked if the therapy was still helping and I said yes in a tight voice. It had been years since he had mentioned it. Whenever the subject

121

came up in the past, I'd felt a shortness of breath. I could feel it now, and he seemed to recognize my silence, so he didn't press the issue.

"Good, that's good," was all he said.

I stared at the water for a long moment and felt that the call was winding down. My father cleared his throat then and said in Mandarin that my mother had contacted him asking how she could reach me. He said this in a low voice. As far as I knew, this was the first time he had heard from her in years.

I had difficulty getting my words out.

"I just thought I'd let you know," he said, trying to fill the silence. We said goodbye after that and I remained on the bench for a while, not doing anything. The water looked very clear as it tumbled over the rocks. I retrieved a journal from my handbag and tried to write something, but my mind felt like cold gelatin. I sat there for thirty minutes, trying to pull words out of my skull, but the effort was painful. Eventually I put the journal back and walked home, feeling shitty.

Inside, I fanned myself with the fedora and stirred honey into a mug of herbal tea. Greedo was playing with one of my socks. I reclined on the couch and opened up Instagram. There was a poet I followed, *@Bella_Writes*, that posted writing prompts on her account. Today's prompt was "crushed material", featuring an illustration of a puddle of shattered glass. I opened my journal and wrote down "crushed material" at the top of a new page. I stared at the page, feeling distracted by something I couldn't name, before setting the journal down and returning to Bella's Instagram. I clicked onto the tab that displayed her tagged photos and examined a recent photo of her at an open mic night in London, the United Kingdom.

The microphone looked like it belonged in her hand. She looked exactly like the person you'd cast in a movie about an edgy poet. I compared every physical detail about her against myself, which I knew was childish. This happened every now and then. I circled back to check if there were new pictures of her and wondered what her life was like, imagining all the ways it was better than my own. People like Bella didn't feel real. When I finally clicked out of her profile, I noticed that I had a new notification.

Brenna French is now following you.

Before clicking onto Brenna's profile, I clicked onto my own to see if there was anything embarrassing. Given my habit of hibernating from social media on a whim, my posts were both few and inconsistent. Most of the posts that had my face in them had long since been deleted. Mostly it was Greedo, hiking trails, and the poems I sometimes wrote for Bella's prompts. I thought about deleting the poems before Brenna had a chance to read them. There was only one picture left that showed my face, but it didn't show enough of it for me to hate it. In the end I didn't delete anything because my curiosity for Brenna's page got the better of me.

Like me, she didn't seem to be the most frequent poster. Unlike me, however, she didn't seem to be ashamed of her appearance. In the first picture she made a sardonic, closed-lipped expression toward the camera that told me she wasn't self-conscious. I scrolled through the feed, looking for new information about her life. There was a picture from two years ago that I paused at, because she was dancing with some guy at a country bar, throwing her hair back and laughing. I looked at the picture and assumed that, for absolute certain, they must have fucked. I did that sorta thing a lot. I kept scrolling until I reached the end of the feed, which was an Ice Bucket Challenge video with the caption "Howdy Instagram!". I recognized Mr. French as the one holding the bucket, but Brenna looked different. Skinny and wild, with none of her sarcasm.

By then, my tea had gotten cold. I sighed, getting to my feet and placing it in the microwave.

*

On my first day I lost a patient, which was never easy, but which I thought I processed well. It was something I'd experienced hundreds of times by now, maybe thousands. Malik, one of the nurses, found me taking a deep breath out on the terrace and asked if I was okay. The terrace offered a beautiful view of the city and its surrounding mountains. The sky didn't have a single cloud. I followed Malik back inside, where the familiar currents of the ICU swept me along.

The week felt like a slog when I was in it, but by the end it seemed to have rushed by in a blur. Everyone had made me feel welcome and the hospital itself, tucked into the pine forest and overlooking the city, was gorgeous. I took my breaks with Malik and we insulted each other's music tastes. The Covid situation seemed to be plateauing in the local area, he said, although on Wednesday we had a man burst into the reception, throw himself to the floor, and start exaggeratedly coughing so that he could jump the line. I'd experienced something similar in Phoenix a few months ago when admissions were at their highest.

Brenna sent me a DM on Instagram asking how my first week had gone. I didn't mention the patient I lost on the first day, or the drama surrounding the man demanding instant Covid treatment. Whenever someone who wasn't a nurse asked me about work, I never went into detail. I told her it was fine and thanked her for asking.

After that we continued to message each other intermittently. Brenna sent me WW3 memes and I replied with cat ones. We didn't have substantive conversations so much as little exchanges like these. Since we refused to admit that the other person was funny, we fell into a habit of responding to each other with hyperbolic, all-caps exclamations like "LMAO I'M SCREAMING" or "ABSOLUTELY DECEASED". I liked to think we were being very satirical and clever, knowing that on the opposite end, the other person was writing these messages with a blank, emotionally-dead face.

LOL I CAN'T EVEN, I replied to the latest post she sent me.

DYING RN.

CATATONIC.

I'M IN NARNIA.

I couldn't help it then. I let slip a genuine laugh and instantly felt ashamed, even though Brenna wasn't there to witness me breaking my cover. Malik looked over at me and raised an eyebrow.

"Was that an actual laugh I just heard from you?"

"My friend, she's an idiot."

"Wait, you have friends?"

The next two weeks passed like this- comfortable but completely without note. I worked, I ate, I slept. On my days off I explored the local trails, read books, and spent too much time on social media. I didn't hear from my father or from Jim Groff. Brenna sent me random things she thought I'd be interested in. Greedo tested my patience. I got my groceries delivered to the apartment and I didn't interact with anyone face-to-face except when I was at work. Now and then I tried to write some poetry, but I didn't try too hard. Sometimes I dressed up even though I wasn't doing anything social. The cubed spaces in my double-sided bookcase began to fill with potted cacti and I gazed at the now mostly-complete apartment with a vague sense of: *this is alright*.

Eventually, I got a message from Brenna that wasn't a meme of some kind.

Hey, we're hosting a little cowboy poetry thing at the saloon tomorrow night. Thought you might be interested. You're a poet, right?

It was past midnight and I didn't know how to reply. I fell asleep looking at the message and remembered it while on my shift the next morning. My first thought was: *she's checked out my profile and, oh shit, she's read my poems*. My second was: *she must be wondering why I'm leaving her on "seen"*. My third was: *I'd love to go, but I can't*.

I spent all day worrying about how to respond, and then worrying even more about taking so long to do so. I started typing something, before deleting it and going over to my profile to reread the few poems I still had up there. The last poem was a short piece about a migration of birds across the Puget Sound, although it was really about my mother. I wasn't kind to myself as I reread each line ad nauseam.

"You okay?" Malik said.

"Yeah, super," I said distractedly. He nodded and left. Break was over. I went back to the conversation thread with Brenna and typed: *Sorry, can't*.

*

I felt shitty for a while. Brenna saw my message but didn't respond, which could have meant either nothing or everything. Dr. Kauffman had told me several times to stop assuming too much in these types of situations, but I was a serial offender. I went to bed early that night and spent my day off wallowing in self-pity.

A couple days later, I got a message.

No big.

I was relieved, but also paranoid that we had lost something. I didn't know what to say, or if I should go back to sending her cat memes, so in the end I didn't say anything. Everything I could think of made me feel self-conscious.

I thought of asking for Malik's advice, but so far my new colleagues still thought I was semi-normal, so I didn't. My next meeting with Dr. Kauffman wasn't until Friday, so I couldn't get her take.

It was entirely possible, I realized, that I was panicking over absolutely nothing at all. Dr. Kauffman could attest that I had a history of creating problems for myself, often to the detriment of my personal relationships.

I was trying to distract myself one night with a YouTube channel devoted to unsolved disappearances, when my phone buzzed and I noticed Brenna's name.

Hey, let's go for a walk sometime.

Yasss, I replied straight away.

Cool. I know some trails around the river. Figured that way we can hang out in a way that's safe.

How sweet of you.

Just taking my responsibility as your only friend seriously. Can't have you going stir crazy now.

I didn't know whether to act flattered or offended, but in the end I settled for just asking her when she was free. It felt like a long time since that day at the bar. The fast pace of the ICU, and the many different faces I interacted with there day to day, always made time seem vast when I looked back on it.

"That's something I actually like about my job," I said to Dr. Kauffman. "It forces me to adjust to changes quickly. I feel like I've lived here longer than I have."

"Yes, I see what you mean."

"And when I'm in nurse-mode, there's no room for my anxiety. I'm not trapped with my thoughts, which I think is very good for me," I said. I waited for Dr. Kauffman to say she was impressed with my self-diagnosis.

"You're a reflective person. That's not a bad thing."

"What I'm saying is-"

"No, I understand. The nature of your work requires your complete focus."

"Yes. I like not having to think too much."

"Why do you think that is?"

"Because when I think too much, I go crazy. I overanalyze every little thing. I'm too sensitive and I hate that about myself. That's why I prefer being at work. In the ICU, I'm focused on the patients. At home, all I end up doing is thinking about everything that's wrong with me."

"Let's change that."

"How? By increasing the dosage again?"

"This isn't something that medication can solve. You know that, Audrey. The pills are there to stop your mood from fluctuating. They can't change how you think."

I sighed. I'd been on Citalopram for over two years now, and I still couldn't tell if it was worth it. Dr. Kauffman was talking about self-love. I was a good person and a damn good nurse, she said, so I needed to be kinder to myself.

"I'm interested in what you do when you're not at work," she said. "Because I think a few changes in habit could make a world of difference."

I didn't mention the crime documentaries I watched, because I knew she'd psychoanalyze the shit out of it. The last time I made that mistake, Dr. Kauffman suggested that I was drawn to stories about young women going missing because I myself was a young woman that traveled alone. It was true that I wondered sometimes if anyone would miss me- or even notice- if something sinister ever happened, but I didn't have some repressed death-wish.

"Not much. I can't exactly go to concerts. But it's fine."

"You say that," Dr. Kauffman said. "But it's not fine. You often say that you don't like people, or that you prefer being on your own, but I don't think that's true. You're just used to it. It's the same with other patients. A lot of them say that they're introverts, or that other people make them depressed, but the truth is everyone needs a social life of some kind. I know that you not letting anyone get close is your way of protecting yourself. You've learned not to become dependent on people. But we've seen before that when you do let people in, it makes you happy, haven't we?"

I shrugged, making a neutral sound.

"I think you actually form quite strong attachments."

"You say that like it's a good thing."

"You seem to think it's a weakness. It's not. You care about people and know how to make them feel valued. People enjoy your company- that's obvious from everything you've told me the past two years."

I was feeling drained already. I checked the time on my screen and decided to tell Dr. Kauffman about the walk I had planned with Brenna later.

"Oh, that's a wonderful idea!" she said. I knew she'd be all about it. "You won't have to worry too much about Covid, being outside."

"That's the idea," I said. I wanted her to think that I'd come up with it, since that would make me look proactive, and like I was implementing her advice. We signed off and I took a shower. Dr. Kauffman's words had a way of making me feel heavy. I tried to believe her assurances that my habit of overanalyzing everything was not, in fact, unique to myself. But soon I felt her words exit my body, as though the memory of our session were a hard block of ice that the shower was in the process of melting. There was only the hot spray of the showerhead. Even after I was clean, I stood there for a long time.

When I went to text Brenna that I was ready I noticed that I had a new message from Jim Groff.

Don't like me, huh?

I met Brenna on the street outside. She was wearing leggings and a college t-shirt, her hair in a high bun. No makeup. Her skin looked pale, but not in an unhealthy way.

"You're not wearing plaid," I said. "Isn't that, like, your whole identity?"

"You look different too," she said. "Though I can't put my finger on it."

"More tired, probably."

We walked to the river and I showed her the message I'd gotten from Jim. Brenna asked me why I hadn't blocked him.

"I don't know," I admitted. "I honestly don't. I keep telling myself I should, but I never go through with it. Every once in a while, I go onto his profile and read through his deranged posts. He literally posts every day."

"Trump supporter?"

"Yes, but more than that. It's almost like he's a satire of the whole thing- except he's not. He says things that I can't imagine another human being actually saying without irony. Conspiracy theories, culture wars, or random unhinged rants about things from his life. I don't know why I keep reading it. It's like I *want* to make myself mad. Do you ever do that?"

"What, as in that specifically?"

"Sure, or anything you know is unhealthy or pointless."

"I guess so. Every now and then I'll get sucked into a toxic comment section or something. But then I realize what's happening and stop myself."

"When I read his posts it's like I'm looking through a window at a parallel universe, where nothing makes sense. It's fascinating in this unsettling kind of way."

We reached the old railroad bridge and crossed over to the quieter side of town that always intrigued me. I found it strange that Brenna felt like a close friend, even though we had only really hung out in person once. It was difficult to know where this inexplicable trust had come from. I talked without thinking through what I was going to say, and when there were pauses, I didn't feel the need to fill them.

"Can I ask about your poetry or is that not allowed?" she said. We were walking under a wooded path on the other side of the river, same direction. It felt cool there and the canopy was filled with a fresh, nutty smell that I liked.

"It's not allowed, but I'll make an exception for you."

Brenna asked me what I wrote about, and I said, "My life", which I was worried would sound pretentious. As though my life were interesting and important enough to be worthy of a poem.

"Ah, I thought you were a nature poet or something."

"Why? Do I give off hipster vibes?"

"You do- but that's not why," Brenna said. She mentioned the poem I'd posted on my Instagram, about the birds migrating away from Puget Sound. The birds were flying west, which was where Taiwan was.

"It's about my mother," I said. There was something about Brenna that made me feel very confessional, I realized. So I told her about the birds flying west, and how my mother had left us when I was fourteen. I told her about my father, who had grown so Christian that he'd lost whatever personality he once had, and the man from Taipei that visited Seattle on a business trip, taking my mother home with him. And then the empty years that followed.

Brenna was a good listener. She reacted to each detail the way you wanted someone to, silent when you needed her to be silent and sympathetic when you needed her to be sympathetic. I soon realized that I was capable of saying anything, absolutely anything, to her- which probably wasn't a good thing.

For the rest of the day, I felt like I was on a high, and I messaged her that evening to thank her for her company. I knew even as I typed it that I probably sounded needy as heck, but I didn't care.

Gross, she said, and I replied with a GIF of a smiling Golden Retriever. She didn't reply to this but I didn't feel insecure the way I might normally have. That evening I switched the fairy lights on and checked Bella's Instagram. The prompt that day was "underbelly". I opened my journal and sat there, waiting.

*

Feeling bold and a little crazy, I asked Brenna that weekend if I could photograph her by the river.

Why??

Bc you're a whole aesthetic.

We met up a few days later when we were both free and this time Brenna was what I liked to consider her quintessential self, dressed in a plaid flannel, jeans, and leather boots. A ring piercing in her left nostril. Her chestnut-brown hair was tied in a fishtail braid and she had just a subtle amount of makeup.

"So you're a photographer as well as a poet? On top of being an essential worker on the front lines of the pandemic."

"When you put it that way, I sound like a superhero."

"Then I said it wrong. What do you want me to do?"

I had her pose on the rocks, right next to the water, with the railroad bridge and the mountains in the background. It was fun bossing her around. She sometimes made a sarcastic quip or raised an eyebrow, but she went along with all of my directions. Even better was Brenna's uncanny instinct for knowing how I wanted to capture her. She had a natural, relaxed expression that seemed to substitute for a smile, with no lines or tension in her face.

Afterwards I told her that she was a great model and Brenna asked me if I was collecting evidence that I had indeed made a friend in Colorado. I called her a bitch and we made plans to go hiking the weekend after next.

*

Before the hiking trip could happen, I ended up testing positive for Covid. At first, I was depressed because it seemed like I had been gaining momentum both at work and in my social life. Then, when the symptoms got worse, I didn't have the energy to think about it in emotive terms. I just wanted to stop coughing. On the whole, my symptoms weren't awful- mostly I just felt drained and weak.

I lay on the couch feeling useless, spending all day in my pajamas and drinking ginger tea after ginger tea. Greedo regarded me unsympathetically and made a whining sound. Maybe he was coming down with it too. I'd read a story online about a cat contracting the virus on the east coast.

The third day was the worst. It felt like innumerable pins were prickling the inside of my throat, I hadn't slept much the night before due to repeatedly coughing myself awake, and to top it all off I was out of ginger root. Social media made me even more depressed than usual, but there were few other ways of passing the time. I was watching news coverage of the president being discharged from hospital when Brenna texted me.

You awake?

Sadly yes.

Brenna messaged me again five minutes later, telling me that she had left a care package outside my door. She wasn't there when I stepped into the corridor. On the floor was a paper bag and a large ceramic tray wrapped in foil. I carried them inside and checked the bag first. Inside were painkillers, cough drops, several cans of tomato soup, as well as bread and cheese so I could make grilled cheese sandwiches. Then I checked the tray. Under the foil was the biggest lasagna I'd ever seen. A post-it note told me to heat it up for thirty minutes. I placed the lasagna in the fridge and returned to the couch, picking up my phone.

What the fuck.

Get well soon.
I actually love you.
Let me know if you need anything else.
Gurl, this lasagna is fkn humungous!!

I was seized then by a coughing fit, but it didn't hamper my giddiness. When I dipped my grilled cheese into the tomato soup later that day, tears welled up in my eyes. I cried a lot over the slightest things, but this time I wasn't embarrassed about it.

Three days (and several lasagna portions later) I was starting to get my energy back. The cough was still there but it wasn't as intense. Brenna came by with another care package, even though I didn't need anything. I stuck my head out the door and waved down the corridor to her as she exited the front entrance. One of the items inside the bag was ginger root, so I immediately boiled some water and started chopping a few slices. The care package this time around was filled with comforts rather than necessities; Funyans, body lotion, bath bombs, and a small box of edibles from a local dispensary. A post-it note told me to try the edibles with the bath bombs.

This is too much!!

Ah, it's nothing. You've been taking care of everyone since Rona began. Someone has to take care of you.

*

The following week I tested negative and went back to work. I was glad to be back in the ICU, because the election coverage was ramping up and the whole thing was driving me crazy. Brenna said she knew something that would take my mind off things and asked if I was free on Saturday. I wasn't, but I was able to get Malik to swap his Sunday shift with me. As I went to reply to Brenna, I noticed that I had a new message from Jim.

You can't ignore me.

It had been a long time now since the day I'd given Jim a ride into the city, and I wasn't sure I would even recognize him if I saw him on the street. He was just a name on a screen that popped up on random occasions. I wondered if maybe I was the same to him- not a real person, who might be affected by these messages, but a simple string of digital characters on a screen. I had to imagine that when he typed these messages, he was doing it thoughtlessly, releasing them into the ether to see if anything happened.

When I got home, I saw that he had sent another one.

You should post more pictures.

After that, another.

Post one of you in glasses.

And one more before I went to bed.

Hahaha are you shy.

Still, I had no intention of responding, and still, I couldn't bring myself to block him. I wondered what the necessary things were that had to happen in Jim's life to lead him to having a one-way conversation with a woman half his age on the internet. A woman closer to a stranger than a genuine acquaintance. Was my inbox one of many that he tried? Or was there something special about me, that even he couldn't understand?

His profile revealed few answers. Jim posted multiple times a day, although most of the posts were shares from conservative media outlets. Tonally they fell into two camps-smug memes about how everyone else was a sheep or unhinged tirades at the supposed cancelling of Christmas.

I stopped scrolling, feeling frustrated. What I wanted was something real; an old photo from his school days, a tribute to a deceased relative, a happy birthday message appended with a reference to an amusing memory. Even when I checked his Basic Info page, it read only "Works at: self-employed" in infuriatingly-vague lowercase. There was nothing- anywhere- that hinted at a real life with complex emotions, despite how active he was on the account.

As the weekend drew nearer, my mood began to deteriorate. I realized that, while I was better, the virus had left me feeling exhausted. A job that was already physically and mentally demanding now felt orders of magnitude worse. When I got home, I was too tired to cook or meal prep, so I survived on consecutive takeout orders. I felt too weak and depressed to write, read, or go outside, so I either spent my free time sleeping or scrolling mindlessly through social media.

Saturday came and I felt like telling Brenna that I couldn't make it. The plan was to hit up an outdoor blues concert in one of the city parks, which she had correctly guessed was totally my jam, but we would be going with her friends, which was low-key terrifying. One thing I'd discussed at length with Dr. Kauffman down the years was how easy I found it to chat to individuals compared to how difficult I found it to chat with groups. Aside from the fact I felt like garbage, I was anxious about Brenna witnessing what was likely to be a 180-degree shift in my personality.

I was trying on a leather jacket in the closet mirror when Brenna sent me a message saying she would meet me at the park, since she was already on the other side of the city. Groups that all already knew each other were scary enough, but having to approach them alone was even

137

worse. However, I knew that staying home meant more junk food, more social media, and more self-loathing. Sighing, I removed the leather jacket and swapped my summer dress for khaki cargo pants and a black, unremarkable men's polo shirt. I didn't feel like doing makeup, so I tied my unwashed hair into a low bun and left.

As I expected, Brenna's friends were all nice people, which made me feel bad about not liking them. I tried to be nice back, but everything I did I felt self-conscious about. I offered forced, closed-mouth smiles and generic conversation. Most of the evening I didn't look anyone in the eye or attempt anything in the way of humor. I knew that Dr. Kauffman would probably tell me that I chose to be miserable, but it was easier to blame Brenna's friends than myself.

"Audrey's a poet," Brenna said at one point, and I felt everyone's eyes settle on me. They made interested noises like "ooh" and Brenna's face relaxed into a self-satisfied smile, as though she had expected that reaction.

"Not really," I said. "I haven't published anything."

"Yet!" one of Brenna's friends said. Why I had the capacity to find this annoying, I had no idea.

"She's really good, too," Brenna said, drinking from her beer and keeping her eyes on mine. I stared back at her open, easy face, conscious of her long eyelashes, and felt a profound sense of self-hatred.

If Brenna did notice any difference in my behavior, she didn't show it. She continued having a good time while I wallowed in self-pity, exiling myself to the periphery of the group and angling my body away from them. The local bands performing in the park's little amphitheater were good, but I wasn't really listening to them. Instead, I was listening to Brenna laughing at something one of the burlier guys was saying.

It struck me then that she was a consistent person in a way I was not. Brenna was effortlessly herself, no matter who she was with, whereas I was a different person depending on my company. I had wondered if our banter was evidence of a special chemistry between us, but as the night went on, I began to think that I wasn't very special at all. I was one of many, and the Brenna I knew existed for everyone else that knew her.

I was thinking about how to make my exit without seeming rude, when one of Brenna's guy friends asked me if I wanted to grab an ice cream from one of the stalls. I hadn't said a word for over an hour at this point, but I forced a smile.

"Sure."

The stalls were arranged to the side of the seats. In front of the stage, a few children and one old couple were dancing on the grass.

"Brenna tells me you're a nurse," the guy said as we joined the line for the ice cream stall. "I can't imagine what that must be like right now."

I was staring over my shoulder at Brenna and the others. By all accounts, everyone was having a great time.

"What... *is* it like?" the guy asked.

I turned back to him.

"Actually, I'm gonna take off," I told him. "Could you tell Brenna I went home?"

The man seemed a little stunned.

"Uh, sure, yeah," he said. I thanked him and left, walking behind the stalls and under the trees, away from the concert. I didn't look back, but once I was far enough away, I slowed down. I kept my ears primed, because I half-expected Brenna to come running after me like a scene from a movie. When I exited the park, I even lingered by the entrance just in case. The din of the music, muffled by the trees, felt like a wholesome echo from the pre-pandemic world.

After a while I started to feel stupid, and crossed the empty street toward my parked car. In my head I could picture Dr. Kauffman's pained smile. *It's always a self-fulfilling prophecy with you, isn't it Audrey?*

*

The next week I skipped my appointment with Dr. Kauffman because I didn't feel like crying. I dropped her a brief email to say I was covering another nurse's shift and stayed in bed, staring at my phone. Nothing happened. I kept cycling between social media apps and refreshing them, but no notifications or messages came my way. I hadn't spoken to Brenna since the blues concert on the weekend, mostly because I was ashamed. Greedo wasn't in the mood for snuggling, so I eventually got out of bed and made a green tea.

As I waited for it to steep, I started to tidy the counter and noticed the edibles Brenna had given me. They came in the form of rainbow-colored gummies and tasted sweet and delicious. After breakfast I popped one into my mouth and waited for my anxiety to dissolve, for the many pointed tips that pricked my chest to soften.

It seemed as good a time as any to reach out to Brenna. I couldn't continue to be passive and rely on her confidence to do all the heavy lifting.

Hey, sorry for running off the other night. Can we talk?

An hour later, Brenna replied.

Working atm. Everything ok?

When do you get off?

I had to wait until midnight before I could see her. Pulling on a crumpled hoodie, I left my apartment and found her waiting on the street, hands in pockets.

"You look like trash," Brenna said. She was looking at my face but wasn't making eye contact. I must have looked exhausted, even though I hadn't done anything all day and didn't feel tired. "You've got bags under your eyes."

"Work's been running me ragged."

I had thought we might walk around the block, but we stayed rooted to where the path to the building met the sidewalk. My arms were folded over my chest, pulling my body into a tight, pointed shape, whereas Brenna kept her hands in her pockets. She looked tired herself.

"I'm sorry. For last Saturday."

"You've said that. What are you sorry for?"

"Just bring miserable and bringing the mood down."

"I had a great time," Brenna said. She studied me closely.

"I've just been really depressed recently," I said. "I hope you don't think I'm antisocial."

"You don't have to apologize for being depressed," Brenna said, her voice slow and considered. "I just thought it would be a chance for you to make more connections here."

"I know. I appreciate everything you've done to help me get settled. I just...it's just that groups can be scary sometimes, you know?"

"I know. But my friends don't bite."

"I know that- at least, on a rational level I know that. I've always struggled to be myself around groups of people, especially when they all know each other. That was the first real social event I've gone to since the pandemic started... and I just wasn't in the right head space for it. I'm sorry."

"You can stop apologizing now."

"Sorry."

"Bitch, I'mma slap you," Brenna said, and we both laughed. She looked relieved that I was finally smiling. We stood in silence for a little while.

"I *would* like more friends."

"No one thinks what your anxiety tells you they do. My friends probably just thought you were shy, which is a pretty normal thing to be in that situation."

"Thanks, that's reassuring," I said. Brenna shrugged. We said goodnight, but just as she turned away, I touched her arm. Brenna turned back. "Also," I said, swallowing, "I think...I don't like sharing you."

Brenna's expression was impossible to read. She just looked me in the eye calmly and nodded. I let her go and we parted ways. That night I slept well, for what felt like the first time in a long time.

*

It's possible I was still high when I'd said what I'd said to Brenna. Either way, I regretted it for the rest of the week. Something in me just wanted to divulge everything when I was around her, despite how needy and petty it made me look.

The week drew quietly to a close, until I was on my lunch break and noticed I had a new message from Jim Groff.

Fucking bitch.

I took a deep breath, staring at the thread for a while, before finally blocking him.

"You ok?" Malik said from across the table.

"Yeah, fine," I answered. I could feel him watching me with concern. "Just beat."

My shift ended at 2am, after 14 grueling hours, and Jim's message came back to me as I drove the empty streets home. At first, I thought I was imagining it, but as I approached my apartment building, there appeared to be someone standing outside the front entrance, peering through the glass. I couldn't get a good look, as the alcove was cloaked in shadow, but I made a snap decision not to go straight to the parking lot.

Instead, I drove all the way to the end of the street, before turning right and then right again, making my way back. When I reached the parking lot from behind, there was nothing out of the ordinary. The streets were still and the presence of trees on either side covered the whole place in darkness.

I switched off my lights and turned into the lot. When I parked in my spot, I noticed that my lips were dry and my heart was throbbing. Even though I wanted nothing more than to be inside, I didn't get out straight away. My eyes examined the shadows of the lot in each of my mirrors, and from my handbag I removed my pepper spray.

Then, sure that the parking lot was deserted, I got out and rushed to the building's rear entrance, fumbling for the right key. The corridor lights came on as I entered. I looked down the corridor, expecting to see a silhouette appear at the other end, but there was no sign of anyone lingering outside the front entrance.

Maybe it was just a drunk person, I thought. I opened the door to my apartment, locked it shut behind me, and loosed a deep exhale.

"Perhaps it was something, perhaps it was nothing," I said to Brenna on the phone the next day. I'd told her about Jim's message.

"Have you had trouble with guys before?"

"Yes, a few times. It's nothing new."

"Me too," Brenna said. "Which is why I say it's better to be too worried than not enough. I'm sure it's nothing though."

"Yeah…" I said. "He's probably harmless. I'm just paranoid that now I've blocked him, he'll come looking for me."

We were quiet for a moment, and I thought back to previous experiences I'd had. A boy in high school that followed me everywhere until I got the principal involved, after which he started to send me violent messages. A friend of a friend that came on way too strong, when I was living in Modesto, California. *Just tell me what I'm doing wrong*, he pleaded, as if he had a chance. A coworker in Eureka with mental health problems, who threatened to kill himself if I didn't go on a date with him. The dozens of guys I'd come across in bars, at events, everywhere from Seattle down to Phoenix. Even when I made myself as small as possible, and made sure that it was unambiguous that I wasn't interested, they kept coming. It sounded like Brenna had some stories of her own.

"If it will make you feel safer…you can stay with me for a few days," she said.

"No, no, you don't have to…"

"I want to," Brenna said, her voice quiet but definitive.

"What about social distancing?"

"Fuck it," Brenna said. "You just had the virus. You're clear, right?"

I was quiet. I didn't know what to say.

"It'll be fun," Brenna said. "I promise."

"Okay…"

"Just pack a bag and I'll come get you."

"Okay," I said again.

That night, Brenna and I were watching *Anatomy of a Murder* under a throw on her couch. The only light in the entire apartment came from the TV. It was a long film, and it became harder and harder to concentrate with Brenna's arm squished against mine, feeling the rise and fall of her breathing. Sometime after my third glass of wine, I leaned in and kissed her. My elbow knocked over the Tupperware bowl in my lap, spilling popcorn over the throw. James Stewart was making a passionate case about something on the edge of my consciousness. My hand was still on Brenna's neck when I realized what the hell I was doing and pulled back.

"Oh God," was all I said for some reason.

Brenna looked completely disarmed for the first time. Her mouth hung open and she stared at me.

"Oh God," I said again. A complete idiot. "I'm so sorry. I'm just…really attracted to you, okay?"

Brenna brushed a strand of hair behind her ear and pawed clumsily for the remote in the darkness. She found it and paused the movie. Silence hung between us. It was all I could do not to kiss her again. She was wearing an unbuttoned plaid flannel over a gray Henley tank, her glasses wonky, lipstick smudged, and a strand of hair caught in the corner of her mouth. Altogether I thought she looked warm and rustic. Brenna cleared her throat, pulling the rogue strand of hair from her lips.

"It's fine, you just caught me off-guard there."

I went back in, slowly this time, and gripped the collar of her flannel, pulling it upright around her chin. Brenna giggled and removed her glasses. She turned off the TV screen and we were plunged into darkness.

Hours later, in the darkness of her bedroom and inches from her face, I whispered, "You make me feel safe."

*

When I woke up, Brenna wasn't in bed. A pool of light lay on the rumpled groove her body had left in the sheets. I touched it, smoothing out the creases and closing my eyes. When I was happy, I tended to be super-super-happy, and when I was sad, the opposite. Right now, I knew that I was in the former, that the pendulum was about as high as it could get, and that, someway or another, it would swing back down quite soon. The sound of cabinets opening and closing in the next room reached my ears, and I decided to get out of bed to try and enjoy my good mood while I could.

I walked into the kitchen, wearing nothing but my panties and Brenna's flannel shirt from the night before. I was several inches taller than her, but given that I was so skinny and Brenna was imposingly full-figured, the shirt still ended up being too big for me- which was a cozy feeling. Brenna didn't comment on this when she saw me, but I hoped that she found it cute. For her part, Brenna looked chaotically-beautiful as she poured coffee, standing at the counter in plaid pajama pants and the same sleeveless tank as the night before, the top two buttons of the placket undone. Her trademark braid had come loose over her shoulder.

"Do you drink coffee?" she asked.

I came up behind her and hugged her around her midsection, feeling bold and greedy. When I kissed her neck, she made a little noise. Brenna turned around to face me, gripping the counter behind her, and I was enjoying the newly-vulnerable look in her eyes. She opened her mouth to say something, but with my hands on her waist I leaned forward, kissing her deeply and bending her over the counter.

Eventually, Brenna detached, clearing her throat and presenting me with one of the mugs of coffee. I grinned and reluctantly let go of her. This was another way in which I was wildly inconsistent as a person- sometimes my confidence spiked through the roof. It was amusing to see Brenna's lack of composure. I wanted nothing more than to stay like this all day, half-dressed and snuggled together in what felt like the total safety of her studio. But I had work and so did she.

"Can I stay here again tonight?" I said as we stood by the door. I was back in my own clothes, but I continued to wear Brenna's flannel over the top. She made no attempt to reclaim it.

"As long as you like," she said.

After that we started sleeping together, and I spent more time at her place than my own throughout the rest of October, bringing Greedo with me. I missed another appointment with Dr. Kauffman, this time because I woke up late and was too lazy to go back to my apartment. When I told her, Brenna said I should reschedule as soon as possible, even if I did feel happy. Dr. Kauffman dropped me an email asking if I was okay and I said I was sorry, something had come up. It had been a few weeks now since our last session, and it felt like a lot had happened, so I promised to be there the next week.

Perhaps because I was riding a wave of confidence, or perhaps to show Brenna that I could be responsible, I decided to call my father. It would also give me something positive to update Dr. Kauffman with the next week.

I was sat up in Brenna's bed when I phoned him. Brenna placed a mug of coffee on the bedside table and took Greedo with her into the next room, closing the door.

"Audrey?" came my father's voice.

"Hey Dad," I said, still gazing at the door Brenna had shut. "Sorry I haven't called in a while."

"I know you're busy. Is everything okay?"

"Yeah, I just wanted to chat, see how you were doing."

At one point he asked me how my personal life was going. I glanced at the coffee by my side, feeling the words suspended in my throat, before answering that the pandemic didn't afford me the luxury of a personal life. My father was an old-fashioned type that had repeatedly stressed the virtue of hard work to me growing up, but he surprised me by saying in a soft voice, "Don't work yourself too hard. You need to look after yourself out there."

"I know...I am..." I said, just as softly. My eyes felt warm.

Toward the end of the call, he brought up my mother again, saying that she was on his case about wanting to talk to me.

"She says she can't find you on social media."

What my father didn't know was that I'd tracked down my mother on Facebook a year ago, and blocked her before she had a chance to find my profile.

"I'll talk to her when I'm ready," I said in Mandarin.

"Yes, you said that last time. When will that be?"

"Why do you care?" I said then. "She left us, remember?"

"She is still your mother, Audrey. It's important that you maintain a relationship with her."

"I have to go."

"Audrey-"

My coffee was cold, so I took it into the kitchen and heated it up in the microwave. Brenna was scratching Greedo behind his ears. He seemed much more willing to let her play with him than me. I watched them from the kitchen, until Brenna called out, "How did it go?"

"Oh, fine," I said.

*

I was writing a found poem based on the string of messages Jim Groff had sent me, while Brenna talked about the strange mixture of hatred and fetishization that characterized men like him. When you read the messages together, the tone went from light-hearted familiarity to obsessive desire and finally to violent hostility.

"You get a full sense of his psychological profile here," Brenna said as she read the poem. "He reveals his desperation and then when it's unacknowledged, he becomes enraged. I think a lot of women will relate to this. I know I do."

"I'm thinking of calling it 'Unread Messages'. What do you think?"

"Hmm," Brenna said, frowning at the poem. She handed me back my journal. "But you have read them though. I think 'Unanswered Messages' would work better."

I had to get it finished quickly. Bella's prompt that day was "lost & found", and I wanted to upload my post in time for her to see it. Using the hashtag #PromptsByBella, there was a chance for my poem to get featured on her account. When Brenna checked out Bella's account and saw the tagged photos of her, I could tell she was a little jealous.

"Now I know why you want her to see this so badly."

"Shut up."

"Don't let me get in the way," Brenna said, and we started wrestling on the couch. Greedo sprang up from his resting spot and watched us for a while, before trotting off to the bedroom. We were interrupted when my phone dinged a couple times. Brenna had me pinned. Panting, she said, "Go ahead, it's probably her."

She released me and I got up to check my phone. It sure as shit wasn't Bella Sutherland, the poetess extraordinaire that didn't know I existed. Brenna went to check on dinner while I read the name: Therese Hansen.

You live in Colorado now???

I didn't feel like replying, so I put it off until the next day, when I was on my lunch break at the hospital.

Hey! Yeah, I live in Colorado now.

Therese saw my message instantly, and I swallowed as I saw the ellipses appear beside her name.

So you weren't going to tell me? I still have a bunch of your stuff.

I'm sorry for not telling you. I thought it would be best to give you space. You can throw out my stuff, it's not important.

I just thought that after everything, you would at least say goodbye. It's scary when people just disappear like that.

I wasn't thinking, ok.

Same old Audrey.

Therese had a point. I did have a habit of avoiding difficult conversations. I decided to bring this up with Dr. Kauffman during our long-overdue session.

"Hmm," she said, and for a brief moment I thought her screen had frozen, but then she continued, "I can understand why you didn't say anything. You and Therese had decided to break up. You were moving to a new city- a new state- and looking forward to a fresh start. But it's clear that you mean a lot to the people you meet, despite what you may think. I've said this before, Audrey, but you have a way of forming intense, deep connections with ease, so I can see why it might be difficult for those left in your wake to deal with your absence."

"It sounds like you're blaming me."

"I'm not blaming you, Audrey. I'm just saying I can understand the shock of finding out someone you once knew intimately has suddenly moved across the country. I'm not questioning your decision to move. We both agreed that it was the right thing for your mental health to get out of Phoenix."

I nodded.

"I do feel bad for leaving without saying goodbye."

"Have you told your new girlfriend about this?"

"No," I said. "And Brenna's not my girlfriend."

"Does she know that?"

"I don't know. We're just having fun; I don't want to ruin it."

"I understand that- and I'm very happy that you're not alone by the way. But given how things went with Therese and your other girlfriends, it might not be a bad idea to have these conversations."

"What do you mean?"

"I mean that you have a habit of falling head over heels for someone before cooling off just as rapidly. You've said that yourself to me many times. The other person wants more from you than you're willing to give and then you leave. This Brenna sounds like a really nice girl- and it's obvious that she really cares about you- which is why I think you should draw from your previous experiences to communicate with her, and make sure you are both on the same page."

I sighed. She was right and I hated it.

"I don't think, from what you've told me about this girl, that it will be as difficult a conversation as you think."

"Okay, I'll try," I said.

My tone was probably unconvincing, but Dr. Kauffman didn't push it. We took a moment to catch our breath and she smiled into the camera.

"Are you okay?" she said.

"I called my father," I told her. "He asked me if I had any news- personal news- and I said no. What do you make of that?"

"I know you find it difficult to talk to your father."

"I do try. I want him to feel loved, because I know he probably doesn't feel loved by anyone else. It's just difficult to say anything of substance. I always resort to generic, vague comments about work or something."

"Have you ever talked to your father about any of your relationships?"

"No," I admitted. "I'm gay. And I don't think he would take that well."

"Not at first, but we know that he loves you. Maybe there is a chance that he might come around."

"It's not on me to go through the emotional labor of rehabilitating him."

"I know. But what I meant was that through time, when he realizes that you're the most important thing in his life, he might come around on his own."

It was hard for me to imagine. Everything about my father was unyielding, which is what drove my mother back to Taiwan in the first place.

"I've always thought that if I tell him, then that's it, we've lost what little connection we have. I'm not ready to let him go yet."

*

That weekend, "Unanswered Messages" got featured on *@Bella_Writes'* weekly spotlight post and my heart damn near exploded. Bella herself even sent me a private message saying that my piece was a powerful reflection of the psyche that seemed to define the men of the alt-right. As for Brenna, she was ecstatic, insisting that we celebrate with a bottle of wine.

She was reading out the nice things people commented under the post, and I took a deep breath.

"There's something I want to talk to you about," I said. I trusted in the knowledge that every time I had been honest with her before, she had been receptive to it. I told her about Therese's message and my subsequent session with Dr. Kauffman. By the time I had stopped speaking, Brenna's celebratory mood had completely vanished. She sat there for a long time, still holding her empty wine glass, before replacing it on the table.

"Are you saying I should be prepared for you to get bored of me and disappear?"

"I don't want that," I said. "But it has happened a couple times. I never intend it to happen, obviously."

"That's not very reassuring."

"I know, I know," I said. "But I want to be honest with you about my past to reduce the chance of repeating it. You've been so, so sweet to me since I moved here. I don't want to fuck this up."

Brenna sighed.

"Okay," she said. "I can respect that. But I think you'll have to be brave and confront the past if you are going to succeed."

I reached for her hand and she let me take it. For a long time, we were silent, both of us looking down at our hands on the couch.

"How did it end, with Therese?" she asked after a while.

"It wasn't her fault," I said. "I think she found my baggage too hard to deal with. I became distant. And eventually we ended up agreeing to separate."

It had been a clean break-up. A long, drawn-out cooling between us that neither one tried to fight. It was depressing to think about it just running out of steam that way.

"What baggage?" Brenna asked.

"Just…this. Everything that's happened since March."

Brenna waited. There was no good place to start, no one thing in particular that sufficed for a perfect answer, but there was something I knew could serve as the next best thing. I told Brenna that I was used to seeing people die, that I was strong enough to accept it every time I arrived for a shift, but that there was one thing that had broken me that summer.

A twenty-eight-year-old man, the same age as myself, on a ventilator, fighting for his life. He had fought as hard as he could, and I'd fought just as hard for him. In his last moments I facetimed his family on a tablet, listening to their hysterical screams as they watched him die through a choppy, pixelated screen, unable to reach for his hand. When I wrapped him up in a body bag afterwards, all I could hear was the echo of those screams, and I thought about everything he had meant to the people he knew throughout his life.

I'd thought about his birthdays, his pets, his many homework assignments, the words of encouragement fed to him by his elders, his hobbies, his dreams, his bitterest arguments, his failures, his first kiss, his last kiss, and all the rest of it. Everything that made him who he was, and the knowledge he and his family had, in that moment, that it was evaporating before their eyes. I'd fastened shut the body bag on what was, at that point, just rotting meat. The man, as a person, had been relegated to memory. The bag was placed into a freezer truck and the weight of him fell upon those he left behind.

Brenna listened, holding my hand, and when I started weeping, she held me close. It was a hard thing to disclose to people who didn't work in the ICU, but as Brenna caressed my hair, I knew that I had to try.

*

The next day, Brenna and I said we would take it slow and steady. She confessed that she had no idea what we were either, but she was curious what we might become. I started to spend more time in my own apartment again, and while I was there I began to write more poems. Being featured on @*Bella_Writes* had brought an influx of new followers, so now I felt like I had to keep posting my work.

"The world already has a Bella Sutherland," Brenna told me when I said I hoped to get featured again. "Now it needs an Audrey Tang."

I decided I was going to write something for my father and send it to him in an email. Brenna said that she would help me when I was ready to come out to him. In the meantime, I finally finished editing the photos I'd taken of

Brenna down by the river, and got a real kick out of the comments her friends left when she used one of them as her new profile picture.

At work, I told Malik about Brenna and he suggested that we double-date sometime with his girlfriend. November was a crazy month- in the ICU, out of the ICU, and in the nation at large- but I could feel myself growing in strength.

As for Jim Groff- I truly didn't recognize him when he first came in, not until I put him on the ventilator. He looked pale as a sheet and struggled to keep his eyes open. There was no way he had recognized me behind my N95 mask. As I tended to him, he asked me if he was going to die. I said no, that I would take good care of him. And I did.

When I came in for my next shift, he was off the ventilator and sleeping. I kept a close eye on him, and when he stirred awake, I sat next to his bed. He blinked at me, looking a little discombobulated.

"You don't remember me, do you?" I said.

"Hm?" he croaked, coughing. I handed him a plastic cup of water and he drank from it.

"Your car had broken down a few months ago and I gave you a ride into the city. Audrey the nurse, remember?"

Recognition washed over his face, and he sat up higher. I could tell that he was too drained to be embarrassed, to be anything other than himself.

"I'm sorry," Jim said in a weak voice.

I nodded, feeling that he had meant it.

"It's okay, Jim. We'll get you out of here real quick."

Copper Rumors

Terrell scanned the faces outside the arrival gate but couldn't find her. There were few people waiting. An elderly couple standing very still, like they had all the time in the world.

A chauffer with a bored expression, holding a sign. A large woman pacing back and forth as she chatted to someone on the phone, her mask covering her mouth but not her nose. A small child that may or may not have been hers, running in every direction and stamping his feet at the long stands of light. Terrell watched the child. He had a tiny afro and sneakers that had flashing lights in their heels, which might have explained all the stamping.

For a moment, Terrell thought it was himself that he recognized in the kid. Then he remembered who it was.

The little boy ran completely amok, jumping on the floor as though it were ice he was intent on cracking. As though to drown everyone. Just to see what it would be like. Sounded about right, Terrell thought.

He decided not to linger, pausing only at the hand sanitizer station before pulling his case through the exit doors. Virginia was humid at this time of year. He pulled off his mask and wet his lips with his tongue. The sky was cut with ribbons of thin gray clouds that became thinner toward the horizon. Glimpses of blue in between. A muggy breeze washed over him as he eyed the line of cars collecting waiting passengers. Terrell rolled up his sleeves and undid the top button of his shirt, before checking his phone.

A message from Charles.

Msg me when you land.

Terrell replied with a thumbs up before opening the conversation thread with his sister.

Outside, he typed, replacing the phone in his pocket.

Ten minutes passed and her car was nowhere in sight. When the wind blew his shirt against his skin, the fabric was damp beneath his armpits. It stuck for a second. Terrell shifted his weight onto his other foot and opened the conversation thread with Charles again. Charles had seen the thumbs up.

Try not to have too much fun without me, Terrell typed.

Sadie and I are going to watch Parasite again.

Don't let her up on the couch.

Such a grumpy dad.

One of us has to be.

Lol true :P

Wish I was back there…instead of here…

You'll be fine. It's only a few days. Chill.

Terrell paused, loosening a breath. Another twenty minutes passed before the pale brown sedan came into view. The car parked and when Sasha emerged on the other side, she was all fireworks, stretching her face and mock-screaming. He noticed then that she was filming him on her cell phone. It was easier to pretend he didn't notice than to tell her he didn't want to be on camera.

"Long time no see," he said.

"Ain't that the truth. Hey, you need help with that?"

"I got it," Terrell said, popping the trunk and lifting his case inside. Sasha lowered her phone and watched the clip she had taken.

On the drive, they tried to remember when they had last seen each other. They both agreed it was Christmas, but Sasha thought it was the Christmas just gone while Terrell insisted it was Christmas 2019.

"No, I'm sure it wasn't that long ago," Sasha was saying.

"Has working from home warped your sense of time? Remember how everyone was afraid that if I came, I'd give them Covid?"

Sasha frowned. "Really? It's been that long?"

"Yeah. Last Christmas was the first time I didn't celebrate it with you guys."

"Shit, you might be right…"

"It was the correct decision to be fair. I wasn't offended."

"Well, you *do* fly around the world for a living," Sasha said.

"True. But we're all vaxxed now, right?"

"I've only had my first shot."

"Really? I've been double-vaxxed for months."

"Okay, *Mr. Essential*," Sasha said, and he chuckled. There was a long silence before she said, "Um, so Dad isn't vaxxed yet."

"What?"

"Yeah…"

Terrell sighed. His sister glanced at him.

"You know what he's like…he doesn't budge."

Terrell winced. He knew his father's hesitancy wasn't something that could be undone overnight.

"What about Mom?" he asked.

"Yeah, she and I got our shots together."

"And Frank?"

Sasha's lips tightened.

"No idea," she said.

Silence fell upon the car. They kept driving south, the parking lots giving way to woodlands. The grass was a richer shade of green up here than in Texas. A wet, colorless haze clouded the passing shrubs.

"Hey," Sasha said with a grin, snapping the silence. "Guess who called off their engagement?"

Terrell indulged his sister in her roundup of the town's pandemic gossip. She talked breathlessly about the lives of people he either barely recognized or didn't care to remember. Evidently a lot of the people they had grown up with still lived around town. He tried his best to sound interested. He asked follow-up questions about the people involved and he made shocked gasps where he felt she expected them. When she went into a story about two neighbors engaged in a bitter dispute over the future of a lemon tree that straddled their respective yards- both of whom, it seemed, were confiding in Terrell and Sasha's father- Terrell wondered if his sister genuinely believed he cared about the gossip or if she didn't know how else to talk to him. If it was the latter, then he wondered when things had changed.

He looked across at her. She seemed happy. He knew she didn't like talking about the news- especially about the pandemic. His eyes landed on her wrist.

"Hey, nice tat."

"Thanks."

Terrell had already seen it on social media of course. His sister posted just about everything that happened to her, even the miserable things.

"Dad must've loved that one."

Sasha raised her chin as she said, "Well, I'm an adult now. I can do what I want."

Terrell found her little act of rebellion in the form of the small heart on her wrist endearing. No doubt she covered it up around their father.

"You know, after I get fully-vaxxed I want to go traveling," Sasha said then.

"Really? Like where?"

"I don't know. Anywhere, I guess. Anywhere that's different to here. I feel like I haven't seen anything."

"We went to Disneyworld that one time," he reminded her. "When you were, like, seven. You loved every minute of it."

"That doesn't count. You know what I mean."

"Yeah, I know," Terrell said. He looked at his sister. "Maybe you could come down to Houston."

Her expression told him that that was not the kind of trip she had in mind. So far, none of them had ever visited. None of them had even met Charles. Sometimes Terrell wondered if Charles found that weird, even though he had never indicated as such. Charles spoke to his family regularly- a lot more often than Terrell did his own. Charles' mother had stayed a week with them in Houston. His sisters had come to town several times for Astros games, for pool parties, for nights of frozen margs. His old school friends too. At the very least, Charles had to notice the contrast.

"I definitely will at some point," Sasha said. "I just feel like, after the past year and everything, I need to do something for *me*, you know?"

"Of course."

"Self-care is very important."

"I know," Terrell agreed. "So, what kinda place were you thinking?"

"Hawaii or Jamaica...someplace with a beach for sure."

"Both excellent choices."

"Yes, I'm sure you already know," Sasha said in a tight voice. Neither of them said anything then. Terrell looked out the window at the passing trees. After a while, Sasha cleared her throat. "So, I heard that you guys get these... Buddy Passes?"

She wasn't doing a good job of pretending she hadn't rehearsed this particular conversation. She waited for him to respond, keeping her eyes on the road. He noticed that her shoulders were tensed.

"Yeah," he said.

"So, you can just give them out to whoever you want? And they fly for free?"

Terrell didn't say anything. Throughout the whole drive, she hadn't once asked him how he was doing. She didn't ask about Charles' big promotion, about Sadie's recent operation, about the airline. Not even what the weather was like back in Houston right now. He stared out the window, his lips in a thin line. He wished the airline didn't even give out those Buddy Passes in the first place.

"Who has yours?" Sasha said.

"No one."

"Okay," Sasha said. She cleared her throat again. "Maybe..."

"What are you asking me?" Terrell said then, turning to look at her.

"What? Nothing. Just making conversation."

"No, you ain't just making conversation," he said. "Just say what you want."

"Forget it," Sasha said.

*

They didn't say anything until they reached town. Sasha took a route he didn't recognize and he looked at her.

"Frank," she said.

He nodded. Sasha parked opposite a box-shaped house of gray-painted wood. An exterior staircase led to the second floor, which was rented as a separate property to the first. Frank's place. The staircase felt less than 100% secure, its white coating peeling off, splinters poking out of the depressions in the wood. At the top, Sasha knocked on the door. No one answered and she knocked again. After a third knock, a sleepy man that Terrell vaguely recognized answered the door.

"He ain't here," the man said. Further into the apartment, a woman called something. The man ignored her. "Y'all will find Frank at Ricky's place, down the street."

The man closed the door and Sasha turned away.

"I know Ricky," Sasha said. They walked back down the stairs. All around them came the hissing of cicadas. The air was parched and there was no breeze. Across the road, the sun gleamed on the hood of the sedan and Terrell squinted.

They drove to another house one block over. In the driveway there was a white van with no license plate, facing the street. The van's back doors were open and so was the garage door behind it. Sasha strode around the van, toward the open garage, and Terrell followed her. There were three of them sitting in the garage but none of them were talking. Speakers played at a loud volume a podcast in which two men discussed the "fundamental differences" between men and women.

Frank looked up at them as they came into view, his lips curling.

"Hey," Sasha said. "Your roommate said we'd find you here."

"Did you find me?" Frank said.

Terrell noticed his sister's hands fidgeting, folding over themselves before the left hand scratched her neck.

"Didn't Mom tell you that we were picking you up for dinner?"

Frank nodded, his eyes focusing on a thick polypropylene bag with four loops, one on each corner. The bag was empty but Frank seemed to be trying to gauge how durable it was, stretching it into a taut box shape.

"Yeah, she told me."

"So…are you coming?"

Frank didn't lift his eyes from the bag. "I'll be there," he said.

Terrell looked inside the van. Just like the bags, it was completely empty. Frank's friends didn't say anything. They just stared at their phones. The volume of the podcast made it difficult to speak but no one turned it down. The guest was saying something along the lines of "But you can't say that these days…" in an aggrieved tone of voice.

Terrell returned his gaze to Frank and Frank looked up at him.

"Little brother," Frank said. Terrell nodded at him and Frank smirked. There was a pause, Sasha shifting her weight from foot to foot, and Frank returned his attention to the heavy-duty bag in his hands. He flattened it into a neat square. Without looking back up at them, he said "I'll see y'all later."

They both knew that meant they were dismissed. Sasha turned quickly on her heel, almost bumping into Terrell as she did. Frank and the other two men didn't look up as they left. The sound of the podcast receded behind them, confined to the shade of the garage. The bushes and treetops continued to hiss in a somnolent, hypnotic cycle. Above, a shapeless sun prickled on their necks. Neither of them said anything on the drive home.

*

The house had no recent pictures. What few photos adorned the walls had done so for twenty years. A single portrait of Mr. and Mrs. Jones on their wedding day. Portraits of each of the three children as babies. And lastly, a portrait of all five of them together, when the children were toddlers. Mr. and Mrs. Jones offering identical closed-mouth smiles- smooth and restrained. Sasha, only two, looked distracted. The photographer was probably saying something to get her to look vaguely in the direction of the camera. An uncertain, worried look in her large eyes.

Terrell cringed at his own face. He looked like he didn't know how to smile. Even at four years old he appeared self- conscious, a twist in his brow. Frank, however, was giving the camera the most manic, over-the-top smile he could. Bared teeth and wide eyes. Eyes that seemed to stare right through the camera and into the present. Even his smile, Terrell thought, was unsettling.

There were no candid photos displayed anywhere. Such photos did exist, Terrell knew, but they were kept out of sight, tucked away in carefully-arranged albums in a wicker bin in a corner of the living room. The house in general was kept austere and featureless, but always neat. Nothing out of place. Like the photos of houses you saw on real estate websites. The clues about the lives of the particular inhabitants were both few and subtle. The crucifix above the shoe rack for one.

Atop a bureau in the dining room sat an old family Bible. Terrell hated it. He also hated that when his father said grace that evening, Terrell found himself joining in. It was easier just to go along with it for a few seconds, but he'd planned on doing what wasn't easy. He'd planned on sitting there with his head up and his lips fastened shut, right up until the moment actually came. Then, predictably and pathetically, his head had lowered, his lips had formed the words.

Mrs. Jones had made a casserole. Frank's chair was empty but no one commented on it.

"How's work?" Mr. Jones said. It was the first time one of them had actually asked Terrell a question about his life since he had gotten off the plane. Terrell cleared his throat. He knew that it was difficult for his father to talk to him about anything else. So work it was.

Terrell told them about the airline and the challenges brought by the pandemic. He talked about the mask mandates, the difficult passengers, about how most of his friends had been furloughed throughout 2020. The Joneses didn't comment or ask questions. Sometimes his father nodded or murmured in acknowledgement. Eventually Terrell stopped talking.

"How much they paying you now?" Mr. Jones said then.

Terrell told him.

After a long pause, Mr. Jones told him how much money the young guys he trained were getting paid for their apprenticeships. The figure was more than the one Terrell had given.

"And they don't have all that student debt to worry about," Mr. Jones added.

There was another pause. Everyone was bent over their plates except Terrell, even though he wasn't finished. Sasha opened her mouth to change the subject but Terrell cut his sister off.

"My last layover was in Costa Rica," he said, looking across at his father. At the opposite end of the table, Mr. Jones didn't look up from his food. The sides of his hair had grown starkly white over the past couple of years, giving his head a badger-like pattern.

Terrell got out his phone and showed his mom some of the pictures from his trip. She smiled at the photos, saying "mm" now and then.

"It's so beautiful there this time of year," Terrell said. "It's been a tough year for our industry, but layovers like this remind me it's all worth it."

"I recognize her from your Instagram," Mrs. Jones said then, pointing at the woman in the photo standing back-to-back with Terrell in the sea. Terrell and the woman wore black sunglasses and had their arms folded across their chests. They had both opted for a flat, tight-lipped expression of mock-seriousness, as though disappointed in the observer.

"Carmen- my best friend. She was born there, you know? So she knew all the authentic places to get food in San José. It was so good. And we avoided all the tourists," Terrell said, somewhat breathlessly. "You'll have to meet Carmen sometime. She's like family to me."

"How come there are never any pictures of us on your Instagram?" Sasha asked then. "You know, your *actual* family?"

Terrell's breath caught in his throat. This was usually his mom's cue to say something like "Now, now, Sasha…" but she remained silent, which made him wonder if she too wanted an answer to the question.

"It's not that…" Terrell began, but he struggled to find the right words. "It's just that there's a theme I'm sticking to. It's a travel account."

"Sure," Sasha said, smiling at him. Terrell put his phone away and they carried on eating. A moment later, Sasha started telling them about a funny encounter that her boyfriend, Eric, had had at Denny's with an old schoolteacher. Mrs. Jones smiled. She liked Eric. His father ran a concrete business on the edge of town. Now Eric worked there too, taking on the bulk of the management during the pandemic.

Sasha snorted as she laughed at something Eric had said to her.

"You two," Mrs. Jones cooed after she was finished. "When's he gonna pop the question?"

"Not yet," Sasha said. "We don't have enough money. That reminds me actually…"

Nothing had changed, Terrell thought, staring down at his half-eaten plate of casserole. They were at the part of the evening where his sister mentioned something important that she needed money for. She never outright asked for the money, but she kept looping back to the given subject until she got an answer. Their father, she knew, had a lot of money in savings and was due to get an excellent pension from the union. And yet, he seemed to want for few things. As far as Sasha was concerned, that money was just sitting there.

"We're going to get it anyway when he passes away," she had told Terrell once when he'd called her out on it. That had been three years ago now. The pandemic seemed to have changed remarkably little, he thought. Everything in the house looked the same. Everything tidily in its place. Everyone exactly as he remembered them.

This time it was a new car. The sedan was on its "last legs" as she kept saying. Terrell was about to say that it seemed fine to him, but just then the front door opened and closed. Frank stalked into the room, hands in the back pockets of his jeans. He was wearing a white tank top so that you could see the full sleeve of tattoos on both arms, as well as the ones that coiled around his neck. Mr. Jones bristled as he glanced at him. The tank had been deliberate, Terrell knew. Their father admonished many things, but he had always had a particular hatred of tattoos.

"That's how you dress for dinner?" Mr. Jones said, not looking at his eldest son.

"It's hot out."

"Put a shirt on."

"Oh, it's fine, Francis!" Mrs. Jones said to Mr. Jones. For the sake of avoiding confusion, she had always called her husband "Francis" and her son "Frank". As a child, he had been "Frank Junior", or simply "Junior", but Frank had asked them to stop calling him that. "I'll grab you a plate from the oven," Mrs. Jones said, popping into the kitchen. She always did have a soft spot for Frank, Terrell thought. She was about the only person that did.

Frank sat down in his chair, next to Sasha, who had fallen silent. Frank studied her, a smirk playing on his lips.

"What? I interrupt something?"

"No," Sasha said, her eyes fixed onto her lap.

Mrs. Jones returned to the dining room with a broad smile across her face. She laid a plate before her eldest son. "Careful, it's hot," she said. She made to grab the serving spoon, but Frank rested a gentle hand on her forearm before taking it away from her.

"That's okay, Mom. I got it."

His eyes flashed at Terrell and stayed there as he spooned casserole onto his plate.

"Glad to be back here in your old hometown?" he said. Terrell stiffened. Everything his older brother said had a way of sounding like a trap.

"Sure."

"Really? I wouldn't have thought so, looking at your Instagram."

Terrell shrugged.

"I could get used to staying in fancy hotels."

"They're not that fancy."

"They look fancy enough to me," Frank said. He kept his eyes on Terrell as he chewed. He ate loudly and talked as he did so. "And those beaches! Gorgeous. Perks of the job, right?"

Terrell nodded.

"I wouldn't have thought an F.A. had it so good. It's basically a waitress gig, right?"

Terrell didn't say anything. It was hard to look his brother in the eye. Frank laughed.

"Just kidding," he said over a mouthful of casserole. "Don't get your panties in a twist. We should be laughing our asses off. It's a weekend of celebration, right? Terrell's home. Dad's got his big thing tomorrow."

"Remember to iron the suit we gave you," Mr. Jones said. His plate was empty and his knuckles rested on the table.

"Of course!" Frank said. "I brush up nice now and then."

Mr. Jones was quiet. He held his eldest son's gaze for a few seconds before thanking Mrs. Jones for the meal and retiring to the living room. Frank was beaming at each of them in turn. Only Mrs. Jones beamed back at him. A single candle on the table flickered, as though warning them it were about to snuff itself out.

"Anyway," Frank said to Sasha. "I interrupted you."

"It's fine."

"I heard something about a car. Go ahead, finish what you were going to say."

"Drop it," she mumbled.

"What was that?" Frank said. When Sasha didn't reply, he said, "You were about to ask the old man for money, weren't you?"

Sasha's lip trembled.

"What for this time? A new car? Was that it?"

"Frank," Terrell said, but Frank ignored him. Terrell felt his throat go dry.

Frank paused to take a few more restless mouthfuls of casserole. Then he put his fork down and turned toward her. Sasha seemed frozen in place, like a small animal trying to play dead.

"What's wrong with the one you got now?" he asked, and this time he raised his voice to show his impatience.

"Battery," Sasha said.

"Okay, so you don't need a new car. You need a new battery," Frank said. He took another mouthful. The speed at which he ate always disturbed Terrell. Ever since they were little, he had hated watching Frank eat. "Why don't you let me have a look at it, before you go getting your claws in the old man?"

"It's fine."

"What was that?"

"It's fine," Sasha said, a little louder.

"I thought it wasn't fine. That's why you brought it up, right? So is it fine or isn't it?"

"I don't know," Sasha said.

"Your brother's trying to help, Sasha," Mrs. Jones said. "He knows a lot about cars."

"That I do," Frank said, flashing his sister a grin. "You know you could save a lot of money if you just asked me for help, right?"

Sasha nodded.

"Okay?"

"Okay," she said.

"There we go," Frank said, leaning back in his chair. His plate was empty before Terrell's was. "That wasn't so hard, was it?"

*

There was no trace of Terrell and Frank in the bedroom they had once shared. The walls that had once been adorned with crudely-taped posters of rappers and MMA fighters were now bare, freshly-painted in olive green. The two desks had been condensed into one, with a neat stack of brown envelopes. The video games had been exchanged for books and plants. The twin beds replaced with a queen. Charcoal-gray sheets and white pillows. The skirting board, doorframe, and windowsill had all been given fresh coatings of white paint. The order of the room concealed the disorder of its history.

Terrell lay in the new bed that night, texting Charles.

I hate it here.

Need a call?

No, let's text. Walls are thin.

Ok.

They're insufferable, all of them. I don't know why they always guilt me into coming home. They don't seem to enjoy my company much. Or even give a shit about me. They didn't even ask me about your promotion.

Lol, that's not a big deal.

You worked your butt off for that promotion.

Yeah, but they don't know me. It's not that weird they didn't ask.

We've been together for three years now. You'd think they'd ask something about you.

I wouldn't focus on it. Every family is different.

Don't go quoting Tolstoy again.

I wasn't going to.

They annoy me so much. And what's worse is that I hate myself when I'm around them. I regress to my teenage self whenever I'm back here. You wouldn't wanna date me if you could see it. I always come back hopeful, imagining that the me that you see (the real me!) will assert itself when I get here. I imagine talking with my family as equals, chatting easily the way that I chat to everyone else. But no. No matter how happy I am or how well things are going for me, I'm crushed into my sad little past-self when I get here. The hope doesn't last long when I get off the plane. Pretty soon I remember why I left this shithole. Because I knew that I was incapable of growth in this place.

Hmm. I understand how a certain place can make you feel that way, but I'm skeptical about things being as set in stone as you think.

I just slip into this lesser version of myself. I feel shitty here. And idk why anyone even cares whether I'm back or not. I don't seem to have any impact on them.

I think they appreciate it. Maybe they're just not good at showing it. Not everyone is.

Maybe. Idk.

Before he went to sleep, Terrell scrolled through his Instagram feed. It was true that all of his pictures subscribed to a theme. Each post had been carefully curated to fit with the others, resulting in a satisfying grid of pale blues and lush greens. White sand and cloudless skies. Terrell himself was in most of them, modeling for gifted sets of swim shorts. Vibrant reds and blues and yellows. His friends often commented with fire emojis. Other comments asked him if he wanted to collaborate as a brand ambassador. Even the photos and reels he uploaded that featured Charles and Carmen were made to fit the theme.

Terrell clicked onto his sister's profile. On her story, Sasha had uploaded the video of him walking towards her car with his luggage at the airport.

Terrell's back in town!!

As he re-watched the story, remembering how sweaty he had been, how he had suppressed his annoyance with her lateness, he wondered if she had really been as excited to see him as the video suggested. No doubt her friends had reacted to it with messages saying how sweet it was, the way they did to the selfies she posted with their parents. Terrell knew how a picture could conceal a hollow center.

He placed his phone on the bedside table then and rearranged the shadows around him into the room as it had once been. Frank complaining to their parents that Terrell had wet the bed again. Mr. Jones sitting on a chair between their beds, reading them a bedtime story. Frank always falling asleep first. The time Sasha had started crying because of Frank's "No Girls Allowed" rule when they were playing on the PlayStation 2. The way Terrell's music stopped playing when Frank came home. The rustling sounds that sometimes came from Frank's bed after he turned thirteen. The bruise Frank had given him when Terrell once said to their parents it sounded like he was keeping a nervous rabbit under the sheets. The way he would wake up some nights in his late teens and discover that his brother's bed was empty.

*

When Terrell woke the next morning, it took a long minute for the room to become unfamiliar to him again. Had his father came in at that moment and told him to get ready for school, he felt as though his body would have effortlessly slipped back into its old rhythms. It was all muscle memory. Within an hour he would be back on the school bus and the decade of college, moving to Houston, working for the airline, and living with Charles, would all fade away as a distant dream. Within minutes he would be arguing with Sasha about her taking too long in the bathroom.

But his father didn't open the door. And as the daylight revealed the new lines and shapes of the room that was no longer his own, the present came back to him.

That day, Terrell took Mr. and Mrs. Jones to lunch in town. They ate at a family restaurant they had often chosen for special occasions growing up. Terrell was surprised it was still going.

"So many restaurants back in Houston went out of business last summer," he told them. He didn't think a little family-owned place like this would be the type to make it. And yet it looked more or less as he remembered. The staff were different, the menu had a few changes, and the tables were arranged in line with social distancing, but the overall vibe was the same.

They ate light on account of that evening's plans. A Greek salad for Terrell and Mrs. Jones. A club sandwich for Mr. Jones. Terrell looked across the oilcloth at his father, the way he picked at the sandwich. It was hard for Terrell to imagine the man functioning without his job. He'd probably have a complete identity crisis. If Mr. Jones had had it his way, he would probably have kept working until the day he died. But he had promised Mrs. Jones that he wouldn't go back on his retirement. That, Terrell knew, he couldn't do. His father had only two weaknesses: drink and his wife. Either one had a way of eroding what he worked hard to maintain.

The more Terrell thought about it, the stranger the old man seemed. As long as Terrell had known him, Mr. Jones had been determined to present himself as being as normal as possible. He was careful never to be something that others did not expect. He would have been mortified, Terrell knew, at how eccentric his kids thought him.

Presently he fidgeted, eating in a distracted, stop-start rhythm. Terrell and Mrs. Jones acted as though they didn't notice, chatting idly about the restaurant and their memories of eating there.

"My treat," Terrell said when the bill came.

"That's very sweet of you," Mrs. Jones said.

"Thank you, son," Mr. Jones said after a second, as though roused from a nap. His eyes didn't meet Terrell's as he spoke. His father, Terrell knew, was a million miles away.

*

That evening, Mr. Jones was the last to get ready.

"Where's Frank?" Mrs. Jones asked them. Sasha and Terrell shrugged. Their mother blinked at them for a few seconds before going back into her bedroom, closing the door behind her. A minute later she reentered the living room. She came up to Terrell, adjusting his tie as she whispered to them, "When your father comes out, tell him how good he looks."

When Mr. Jones came out, they all complimented him one after another. Mrs. Jones kissed his cheek. The four of them exited the front door just as Frank was walking up the driveway. True to his word, the suit appeared to have been ironed.

"You look like a million dollars, Pop," Frank said with a grin, and Mr. Jones grumbled his thanks.

Sasha wanted to take photos but Mrs. Jones said that there would be plenty of time for that at the dinner. If they hung about any longer, they were going to be late.

On the drive to Richmond, Sasha did most of the talking. For the first twenty minutes, Terrell pitched in wherever he could, before joining his father and brother in silence. A band of deep orange marked the horizon. The hills were dark and the sky was pale. White stars met the silhouettes of utility poles. An isolated tree in a rippling pasture.

Terrell was reminded then of drives to and from the city. How peaceful it could sometimes get when night fell and they were all tired. How they sometimes drove for miles without fighting, without even making a sound. The smooth sound the wheels made on the highway would lull him and his siblings to sleep.

Terrell had always enjoyed trips to Richmond. Or to D.C., to Philadelphia, to Virginia Beach, to all the cities they had visited. The immensity of their structures, the scale. He felt like he was somewhere real for once. A place where important and interesting things happened. A place where he had felt connected to the world at large for the first time.

At the hotel, Terrell was struck by the amount of people that had showed up. He knew that his father was a big deal at the union, but he never expected this kind of turnout. A hundred people or more milled about in the convention room the union had rented out, glasses in hand, most- but not all- wearing face masks.

As the Joneses meandered through the crowd, it seemed tacitly understood that they were there as a kind of prop for Mr. Jones to vaguely refer to. Terrell glanced at Frank, whose face betrayed little except his boredom.

They touched elbows with men in suits and offered obliging smiles at the nice things they said about Mr. Jones. Sasha insisted on multiple selfies, and to Terrell's surprise, Frank played along. Of all of them, perhaps Mrs. Jones looked the happiest. Terrell eyed his father. Mr. Jones took every free moment he could to finish another drink, before smoothing his suit and obliging the next well-wisher.

"And what business are you in?" a man asked Terrell at one point, as though expecting it to be in a related field to their own. Everything about the man seemed to be shaped in quadrilaterals: torso, head, and moustache.

"Aviation," Mr. Jones answered for him.

"Really?" the man said, eyes widening. Terrell knew that he was picturing something like a structural engineer. "Interesting. We'll have to talk about that later."

Terrell made a note to avoid him for the rest of the evening. The dinner was a choice between country ham and mountain trout. Terrell chose the trout and his father went for the ham. Mr. Jones ate in the same stop-start way he had at lunch earlier that day. A few of the older men gave speeches, telling stories about Mr. Jones from when they were Terrell's age.

During his father's own speech, Terrell suddenly realized that Frank was nowhere to be seen. If Mr. Jones also noticed this, he didn't show it. He gave his heartfelt thanks to the union, to co-workers past and present, to his deceased father, and to his family. As Mr. Jones listed their names, Terrell scanned the room. He was still scanning it when it erupted into applause a moment later. He blinked and joined in, the clapping on the periphery of his consciousness.

"Proud of you, Pop," Terrell said, and everything beneath his skin ached to hear it back.

Terrell finished the rest of his champagne and slipped away. Outside, he spotted the same white van he had seen sitting in Ricky's driveway the day before. The backdoors were open once again. His feet came to a stop when he was in earshot. Ricky and Frank must have been looking into the van.

"That chickenshit," Frank was saying.

"So now what do we do?"

"We go ahead anyway."

"Just the two of us?"

"You chickenshit too?" Frank snapped. Ricky went quiet. "Tonight's the perfect alibi. The sooner I'm back here, the better it will be."

Just then, Terrell's phone beeped. Then again. Again and again. He knew without looking that Charles was replying with emojis to each of the individual photos he had sent him during the dinner. It was no use trying to hide. Frank rounded on him from behind the van and fixed him with a look so penetrating that Terrell felt his lungs physically contract.

It was the same look Frank had given him ten years earlier, when he had caught Terrell on his laptop. Frank wasn't supposed to be home. The laptop hadn't meant to remain unlocked after Frank had left it there, but there had been a pop-up for an update that prevented it shutting down. Frank could tell immediately from his little brother's face that it was too late- that the image of the muscular, panting bodies had been seared forever into Terrell's mind. Before anything could happen, Mrs. Jones called from the kitchen, asking for help reaching something on top of the fridge. The two left the room in silence. The beating came later- a wordless pummeling that split Terrell's lip and bruised his ribcage, leaving him unable to breathe for a brief, horrifying moment. Nothing was ever said about what he saw.

Though Frank didn't say as much, Terrell was convinced that his older brother could see the recognition of the memory in his face.

"Get in," Frank said, and Terrell got in the van. He was shaking because he was still there, ten years ago.

Ricky gave Frank a puzzled look and Frank told him to get in too. Frank closed the backdoors, got in the driver's seat, and they left. Just left, without a word. Terrell glanced back at the hotel entrance, imagining what expression his father might have if he saw them, but no one was there.

A short drive took them to a row of warehouses, all of them bordered by chain-link fencing. Ricky got out and Terrell turned to face his brother, who regarded him with a calm expression. Despite everything, it was a face that Terrell loved. He couldn't explain why.

"Turn off your phone," Frank said.

"Why?"

"Just do it."

Terrell turned off his phone.

"Good. Now put on these gloves," Frank said, in the same light, steady voice. He handed Terrell a pair of puncture-resistant safety gloves. "Just follow my lead, okay? All we're gonna do is go into that yard over there and help ourselves to some of the copper they've got laying around. Anything copper, you put in a bag."

Terrell was shaking his head. "I can't."

"You can. You will, little brother. I'll consider it a personal favor. With three of us working, we should be done and back to the hotel before anyone even notices we're gone. Don't worry, there's no security guard. Ricky and I used to work here, before they laid us off last summer. We know it inside-out. Just a scrap yard full of old server bays. It all goes into recycling. They probably won't even know we lifted it."

"Frank-"

"Get out. Now."

Terrell's heart was in his throat, but he knew that he would do whatever his brother told him. Outside it was dark. They tread lightly and only spoke when necessary. A hole had already been cut into the chain-link fence by the bushes. They each carried two of the heavy-duty sacks Terrell had seen the day before.

Inside, the scrapyard was indeed full. The supervisor for the recycling department, Ricky whispered, had ordered more scrap than they had room for inside- especially with the reduction in workers due to the pandemic. So all of the new bays were unloaded directly from the trucks into the yard, sitting there between the skips and the parking lot for weeks on end.

The whole place was a labyrinth of scrap metal. The bays towered over them, some of them half-stripped of their insides already, but most untouched by the workers. All around the floor were sacks containing the parts they had stripped so far. Fiberglass cables, gold connectors, batteries, and RAM cards. Hollow chassis and sheet metal. The aluminum separated from the other metals. And copper.

"Leave the gold," Frank hissed. "Too hard to sell."

The height of the many server bays allowed them to use their flashlights without anyone from outside seeing. Frank and Ricky worked quickly in the dark.

This is ridiculous, Terrell thought, looking down at his suit. How had he been led to this situation so easily? Why had his body- which hadn't been around Frank since before the pandemic- so readily followed his orders? Once again, his regular life felt like a faraway dream. It was pathetic that he could find himself trapped like this after being independent for so long.

Frank gave him a hard nudge and gestured to a sack on the ground.

"Transfer all of the copper connectors from this one into your sack. Leave everything else." When Terrell remained paralyzed, Frank added, "Sooner these bags are full, sooner we get back to the hotel."

Terrell got to work on the sack. Frank and Ricky, meanwhile, started cutting what they could out of the bays. The sacks were heavy when full, and it took two to carry each one back to the van. Ricky had to cut a wider hole in the fence to fit them through.

"Just one more," Frank panted as they hauled the fifth sack into the back of the van. He glanced up and down the road. It was still deserted. "Hurry up."

Terrell wasn't sure how long they had been gone once they made it back to the hotel. His arms ached. Frank was giddy and laughed the whole drive back.

"Told you it wouldn't take long. That's how it goes when you plan things right."

There was no doubt in Terrell's mind that his brother had planned it carefully, probably as soon as he learned their father's retirement party was being held so close to the warehouse. It was a solid alibi. And the yard had been such a mess that it wouldn't be noticeable that some sacks were now lighter, that some bays were more empty.

He remembered then how a schoolteacher had once told their parents that Frank, despite his problems, had a lot of "natural talent". Mrs. Jones had held onto that remark ever since. A child psychologist even said he might be gifted, but recommended medication for getting him to calm down and focus. Mr. and Mrs. Jones refused point blank.

"He's just hyper, that's all," Terrell had heard Mrs. Jones say one time. "School has to slow down for the other kids, and then Frankie gets bored."

Terrell had always had mixed feelings about that one. It might have explained some of the things Frank did, but it felt insufficient. In fifth grade he got expelled for biting the teacher's hand. Was that just a symptom of boredom? Of being too far ahead of everyone else? Terrell didn't think so. But on the other hand, there was a part of him that was desperate to believe that his brother was, in some way, brilliant.

Terrell and Frank got out and Ricky slid into the driver's seat. The two brothers watched him drive away, dust all over their pants. Frank removed a flask from the inside of his jacket and took a long draw. When he finished, he wiped his mouth on his sleeve and extended the flask towards Terrell. Terrell took it in his hand and drank. The whiskey burned his throat but he remained composed, surprising himself.

They entered the hotel lobby and found Sasha waiting for them.

"Where were you?" she asked Terrell, before casting a worried look at Frank. Terrell couldn't think of what to tell her.

"Just went out for some air," Frank said.

Terrell could see that Sasha wasn't buying it. Frank went into the convention room and the two of them lingered at the door. There were less people inside than before.

"Dad's hella drunk," Sasha said, grabbing Terrell's arm. He must have been shaking, because she looked up at him then. "Hey, are you okay?"

"Fine," Terrell said. "Where is he?"

Terrell didn't recognize the uninhibited hyena-laugh that reached his ears, drawing him toward a cluster of men at the far table. He waited for them to disperse, leaving him face to face with his father. Mr. Jones was propping himself against the back of a chair for balance, his shirt half-way unbuttoned and his tie nowhere to be seen.

When he sobered up, he was going to be horrified at the idea people had seen him like this. But his co-workers, Terrell knew, had probably found it endearing. Seeing old Francis Jones finally loosen up. He wished he could make his father realize it wasn't something to be embarrassed about. An early flicker of that embarrassment seemed to cross Mr. Jones' face when Terrell approached him, and he tried to straighten up.

"You were my biggest hope," Mr. Jones burbled. He gestured with his hand and opened his mouth to elaborate, but nothing came out.

"Let's get you home, Pop."

Just as they had so many times before, the Joneses drove south out of Richmond in total silence that night.

*

Terrell didn't see Frank again before he left the next day. When they had gotten home, Frank clapped Mr. Jones on the shoulder and said "Helluva party, Pop," before disappearing into the night. Terrell went straight to bed and lay awake for a long time.

Once more, he half-closed his eyes and tried to rearrange the shadows into the room he once shared with his brother. This time, however, the room eluded him. Everything was blurry. Memories he had once been sure of were now subject to doubt. He had spent so many hours of his life in this room, hours that now felt irretrievably lost.

Frustrated, Terrell closed his eyes. A second later, they snapped open. He remembered that his phone was turned off. He turned it back on and waited. There was a message from Charles.

How'd it go?

Terrell's thumbs hovered over the keypad for a long time. *Pretty uneventful actually,* he replied.

The next morning, Terrell said goodbye to his parents. Their faces seemed to tell a lot. His father, realizing that he didn't know himself as well as he had thought. And his mother, determined to believe in the best version of things no matter the cost. A pair of old fools that he loved.

Sasha drove him back to the airport. During the ride, they talked intermittently about nothing much at all. Terrell could tell that his sister was curious about where he had disappeared to the night before. She opened her mouth and he thanked her, then, for the ride.

"Oh, no problem," she replied in a distant voice. Her mouth closed.

"My Buddy Pass," Terrell said. "It's yours. If you want it."

Sasha didn't seem to know how best to respond. She frowned at the highway ahead.

"Just make sure you do something memorable with it."

Under the Soil

I

Transatlantic sun pouring into a fifth-story classroom. Nervous laughter. Bodies shuffled excitedly from desk-to-desk in a game not unlike speed-dating. Anxious bodies. Damaged bodies. Yearning bodies. Two threads crossed for the first time. One thread carried a history of being ignored and the other a history of the opposite. Both threads were restless, twining briefly at the desk in a smile, a comment, and loosening once more.

II

In a gray, windowless classroom, Chet made for the table in the far corner, taking a seat opposite a tall girl in a tweed coat. As he sat down, the girl offered him a short, closed-mouth smile in recognition that she remembered him from last week's icebreaker session. Bella-something, from Suffolk.

She took a sip of water before reapplying her face mask, her eyes returning to the phone in her lap. Chet noticed that her straightened, neck-length hair was brown at the top but blonde below the ear. He wondered if it was naturally like that or if she had bleached the ends. As they waited for the seminar to begin, Bella absent-mindedly twirled one of the golden strands around her finger.

Chet was in no rush to force conversation. He leaned back in his chair and nodded at those that joined the table, trying to recall their names. By 9am, there were five of them sitting in silence and pretending to read their phones. A few minutes later, their professor arrived flushed and breathless, taking her place at the front. She set a bundle of folders down on her desk with a thud and blinked at the room around her, as though noticing it for the first time.

"Ah, I like this room," she remarked, brushing her hair out of her eyes. "This is where the students that run the university magazine hold their meetings."

Around the walls were smartboards, one for each table. The room was silent. The professor gazed enthusiastically at the waiting faces, still catching her breath.

"I know that many of you have come to this course from a Creative Writing background," she began. "So hopefully you'll all enjoy the exercise I've set you today."

Each table had to choose a book and develop a marketing strategy based on its target consumer.

"This is the kind of meeting that publishers have all the time. I want each group to take on the role of a marketing department and really think about who your chosen book is for. What is its *value proposition?* What design choices will you use to appeal to your target consumers, and what channels will you use to reach them with your marketing campaign?"

the professor said. She took a pause, scanning their faces. "The people you're sitting with now will be the same for the next four weeks. Today's exercise is very simple. I want you to choose your book and construct an image of your book's average reader."

The professor gave each table a series of worksheets stapled together. Chet took it from her and examined the questions above the boxes.

"Are you volunteering to be the scribe for your group then?" the professor asked in a chipper voice.

"Sure, I'm game," Chet said, leaning back in his chair again. "But how specific are we meant to be with this? It says *name* right here."

"Okay, so Chet's asked an important question," the professor announced to the classroom. Bella gave him a brief, disinterested glance before returning her eyes to their teacher. "Your task today is to create the *quintessential* reader for your book. This is an individual- so we need to know their name, their lifestyle, their background- everything. Don't worry if it sounds silly or unimportant- write it down. The more information, the better. You want to be as specific as possible. When I worked at Hachette, we had meetings like this all the time, for every title we brought to market."

There was a buzz of excitement about the room. The professor returned to her desk and logged into the computer, looking like she had a million things on her mind. Little by little, the classroom filled with noise.

"What was y'alls' names again?" Chet fielded to the table, rocking back and forth in his chair.

"Louise," the girl on his left answered decisively. Chet figured her for a Type A Personality. Probably did all the recommended reading. Would likely end up snagging a job at somewhere like Penguin Random House before she even started her dissertation. Editorial.

The rest continued in a clockwise fashion around the table.

"Svetlana."

Chet remembered Svetlana from the icebreaker session. Gold-rimmed glasses, a white buttoned-up blouse with a black neckerchief, and a waistcoat. Left-brain vibes. Focused. Chet thought about it for a few seconds. Rights Management.

"Navamita."

A sunny disposition. Always dressed in colors of the rainbow. Quick to joke around and even quicker to laugh. There was no doubt. Marketing and Publicity.

"Bella."

Bella-something from Suffolk; not shy- just happy being quiet, by his reckoning. There were many layers there beneath the surface, but she didn't just give that shit away. You had to work for it. Chet had no idea- Design maybe? Or perhaps she wouldn't get a job inside the industry at all. She didn't look like the 9-5 type.

"Chet," he reminded them.

"You're American," Navamita observed.

"Yes ma'am. Texas born n' bred."

"But you're not *dressed* like a Texan," she teased.

Chet leaned further back in the chair, enjoying the attention.

"I'm from Houston. We ain't all cowboys, y'know. So, what book do y'all wanna do?"

Bella shrugged.

"What about *Under the Soil* by Marta Kushak?" Louise suggested.

"Oh my gosh, I *love* that book," Bella said.

"I literally cried at the end," Navamita said.

"Me too."

"It's being made into a Netflix series," Svetlana said.

Chet wondered what he could infer about his group members knowing they all adored the novel billed as "*The Post-Brexit Wuthering Heights*". He hadn't read it himself, but he had seen a BookTuber describe it as "overrated". Something about it being marketed as literary fiction despite it reading like a lightweight romance. He didn't dare bring this up though.

"Sounds like we have ourselves a winner," Chet said. "So, what's our reader look like?"

The girls exchanged looks with each other and started giggling.

"Us," Louise said.

"Alright, so our reader is female?" Chet said, writing it down.

Bella slipped out of her tweed coat, folding it over the back of her chair.

"I love your turtleneck," Navamita said to her, the wide smile reforming itself once again.

"Can't have too many, right?" Bella smiled, brushing some lint off of her shoulder. Chet took note of this as he wrote on the worksheet. The tweed coat. The gray turtleneck. The brown hair that became blonde the further it got from her head. That her name was Bella. It all felt familiar, even though he knew it wasn't. It was like she fit a mold he was already aware of, as though she could only exist exactly the way she was right now, with no other version possible.

"How old is she?" Svetlana asked.

"Twenties," Louise said.

"Twenties?"

"Early twenties."

"Never goes anywhere without her tote bag. She loves tote bags," Navamita said.

"Drinks an almond latte."

"Starbucks?"

"Costa."

"I feel attacked," Bella interjected. They all laughed. Chet laughed too, scrambling to get all the details down in the relevant boxes.

"What does she do?" he asked.

"Hmm," Louise said, drumming her fingers on the table. "I feel like she's a teacher."

"Yeah, a Primary School teacher," Navamita agreed.

"Fresh out of her degree, so she's not jaded yet. She loves her job and lets people know it."

"So, she's married to her work?" Chet asked.

There was a pause. Navamita and Bella frowned.

"No…" Bella said, lips twisted in thought. "She works hard but she has a lot of fun on the weekends."

"She loves The Body Shop," Navamita said and the girls burst out in hysterics. Chet didn't understand the reference, but he wrote it down.

"Fuck sake," Bella said, stifling her laughter.

"Probably has succulents along her windowsill," Svetlana said. "And maybe a cat."

"She lives for yoga," Navamita said.

"And wine," Louise added.

"I'm just gonna say it," Bella said. "This girl sounds like such a vibe. I'm liking her a lot."

"I know," Navamita said. "I want her as my best friend."

"What's her socials?" Chet asked, writing as fast as he could.

Louise peered over his shoulder and grimaced at his handwriting.

"Definitely Instagram," Navamita said. "She has Facebook but doesn't use it."

"Twitter?"

"No, she deleted it."

"Tik Tok?"

Navamita paused in thought. "Yes…" she said at last. "But she held out for a while before giving in to it."

"Instagram is definitely her home," Louise said, brushing a strand of wine-colored hair behind her ear. For several seconds the girls watched Chet filling in the boxes on the worksheets. When he was done, he started leaning back on his chair again.

"Instagram," he said. "I feel like she doesn't just consume it. She's a creator too."

The girls looked at him. Chet set the front legs of his chair back on the floor, resting his elbows on the table. "She sounds like the kinda chick with two profiles. One where she posts pictures of her cat, her family, all that personal stuff. That one's private, obviously. But then she has a public account where she posts her poetry."

"Ooh, I like it," Louise said.

Chet continued. "You know the kind I mean? She'll have a schedule that she keeps to and little illustrations she does on her iPad to accompany the poems. Has an eye for design. All the posts will be carefully made so that they look nice together as a block."

The professor was hovering by their table.

"Keep going," she said. "I'm curious about this person now!"

Chet cleared his throat, pretending to think. "In her real life she's quiet," he said. "Everyone thinks of her as the sweet one of the group. Never curses, argues, or complains. Everything about her is neat and ladylike. She's great with the kids at school and the parents feel good about her teaching them. But in her poems, a different side of her comes out."

"Ooh!"

"These ain't pretty little rhyming couplets about nature. These are brutal freeverse poems about the darker parts of the human experience," Chet told the captive audience. "This lady don't hold back. There's a lot of sex and swearing. And taboo. She delights in making her readers uncomfortable, and her followers love that she writes about the things everyone is too scared or polite to discuss in real life. She had a difficult childhood but played the part of the perfect student and the perfect daughter to try and keep things together. Her poems are the product of all the rage she suppressed growing up- and her exhaustion with living up to a certain image for the benefit of others."

"You certainly paint a vivid picture!" the professor said, and drifted off to the next table. Louise, Svetlana, and Navamita were all looking at him with interest, but Bella's eyes were cast at the floor.

"Is she a feminist?" Svetlana asked.

"Absolutely," Chet answered. "The ferocious kind."

"Write that down," Louise said. "I definitely think that Marta Kushak's typical reader is an angry feminist."

"What's her situation though?" Navamita said. "Is she seeing anyone? Is she married?"

"I think she plays the field," Chet said. "I can't see her being the doting wife, even though that's what everyone expects of her."

"I agree."

"So, she's on Tinder?" Svetlana asked.

"Yeah," Chet said. "She dates a lotta people- men and women- and all of them fall head over heels in love with her. But at the end of the day, she's too chaotic to settle down. Doesn't let anyone get close. She's happy with her books and her cat."

"I love her," Navamita said.

The professor signaled that the exercise was coming to an end.

"Shoot, we ain't even got a name," Chet said, looking up at his group members.

"What would be a good name for a bookish Primary School teacher that's also an edgy Instagram poet?" Navamita asked.

"What about Amy?" Louise suggested.

Svetlana and Navamita looked at each other and nodded. But something about the name didn't sit right with Chet.

"I dunno," he said, leaning back in his chair. "It's not edgy enough."

"She wasn't *born* edgy," Navamita exclaimed, laughing.

"Okay, how about the alternate spelling then. Aimee with a double-e."

"Love it, ha ha."

"I feel like we got really specific with our reader," Svetlana said.

"That's what makes it fun."

When the class was finished, the five of them walked together down the stairwell. One by one, the students peeled away, until it was just Chet and Bella. They walked in silence across the courtyard of the John Galsworthy building, through the busy corridor of the Main Building, and out the front entrance, onto the street. Double-decker buses came in waves, some hissing to a stop and others rattling on to the Kingston town center. The sound of a jackhammer breaking up asphalt drifted over the rooftops. Chet opened his mouth to say something but stopped when he noticed Bella had come to a halt behind him.

He turned to look at her. Her posture was rigid, arms folded across her chest, and the only thing that moved was the straight bottom of her hair, billowing gently like a curtain around her chin. It seemed as though the ends had taken on the quality of the sun. Bella looked at him with eyes that didn't flinch, and Chet didn't say anything.

"You don't know shit about me," Bella said finally. She waited a few seconds, holding his gaze, before stalking past him, arms still crossed.

On the bus, Chet opened up Instagram on his phone. When he tapped the search bar, the first suggestion that came up was an account named *@Bella_Writes*. He tapped on the account. The profile picture showed a young, early-twenties woman peering at the camera over the top of an especially large coffee mug.

The most recent post, dated a couple of days prior, was a found poem of overheard conversation fragments from the London Underground. Each line was a glimpse into another life, with enough suggestion that each one was deep and complex in its own way. Each speaker was the protagonist of their own story, which Chet figured was probably the point of the piece. When he thought about it, it was just the same with the seminar he had attended that morning.

A countless multitude of decisions and coincidences in their respective personal histories that had led each of them to that exact moment, at the same exact table. And after overlapping for forty-five minutes, they had just as easily scattered, wholly separate once again.

III

A week later, Bella woke up and blinked at the stands of light creeping through the blinds. She lived in an apartment above a shisha bar with three guys, just down the road from the campus. Even though it only took her two minutes to get from her front door to the university, Bella found that this arrangement made her late more often than she was when she had to commute from New Malden during her undergrad days.

Grumbling, she rolled out of bed and changed into high-waisted jeans and a black turtleneck. In the next room one of her roommates was sprawled on the couch in his boxers. There was a large tattoo of a Xenomorph on his right bicep and his nose seemed to whistle as he slept. On the coffee table next to him were two pizza boxes from Tasty Bite, the pizza joint next door to the shisha bar below them. Bella opened the boxes. The first was empty but the second had one slice left.

Score.

Bella took her breakfast over to the kitchenette, eating the cold pizza slice with one hand and making a cup of herbal tea with the other. As she waited for the tea to steep, she gazed out the window. The apartment had a balcony on the back. It was nothing pretty, but still nice to have. The view was a narrow parking lot, a garbage skip, and the brick façade of the apartment block opposite.

As Bella crunched down on the hard crust of the pizza, a bird landed on the balcony railing. It had brown wings and a dark blue body dotted with white streaks that looked like arrowheads.

Bella took a picture of the bird on her phone and sent it to her grandma, asking her if she knew the species. The bird hopped along the rusted railing, before coming to a stop. It kept angling its head in various directions, but it seemed happy just sitting there. As she stared at the bird, Bella felt a kind of longing somewhere in her chest. It felt like a messenger from a place she would much rather be.

A grunt brought her back to the apartment. Her roommate was stretching out on the couch. Why he hadn't just slept in his room, Bella had no idea. The floor was littered with beer bottles.

"You're a mess," Bella told him, stirring her tea.

The man blinked at her, scratching the hair around his nipple piercing.

"Oh, that's rich coming from you," he croaked.

Back in her room, Bella gulped the last of her tea and gathered everything she needed for class. She was about to leave when she paused at her bookcase. *Under the Soil* by Marta Kushak caught her eye with its turquoise cover, and on instinct she plucked it from the shelf, stuffing it into her satchel.

Her leather boots clapped down briskly on the sidewalk as she hurried toward the campus, and by the time she had reached the stairwell of the John Galsworthy Building, sweat prickled in her armpits. As she huffed up the stairs two at a time, she caught a glimpse of her reflection in the glass. She hadn't had time to straighten her hair, so the blonde ends curled around her jawline like nettles.

"Sorry I'm late," she said to the professor as she entered the windowless classroom.

The rest of her group were all there, arranged exactly as they had been one week ago. She took her seat opposite Chet the Texan, who was rocking slowly on the back legs of his chair again. There was something about it that annoyed her in a way that was difficult to articulate. It was like whistling, cracking your knuckles, or humming a song- all of which she suspected he was also guilty of. An overexposure of personality, probably to hide a lack of real depth.

Maybe it was an American thing. In the U.K. you were encouraged to make yourself small. In the U.S., she suspected, you were probably taught to make yourself big.

As they continued last week's exercise, Chet kept clicking his pen whenever he seemed to be in thought. That was even worse. Bella kept her head down and tried to block him out as best she could, counting down the minutes until the seminar would be over.

Louise was reviewing all their notes from last week.

"I like what you said here," she told Chet. "About all the people she meets falling hopelessly in love with her, but it's always unrequited. It's interesting..."

"I feel like we are writing a novel!" Svetlana said.

"I feel sad for her though," Navamita said. "I want Aimee to find her match."

"She ain't unhappy," Chet replied. "She's just not into the whole commitment thing."

"I love how invested we all are in this character," Louise said. "It's like she's real."

Chet started clicking his pen again. Bella stared down at the cover of *Under the Soil* in her satchel. The illustration showed a clenched fist, soil pouring through the cracks between the fingers. What looked like a cut on the knuckle. Bella took a deep breath.

"I think..." she began, and the rest of the table turned toward her. Chet stopped clicking the pen. "I think Aimee attracts a lot of the wrong guys, you know? Guys that think they know her, that tell her they want to get to know her, even though in their mind they've got her all figured out."

"Ugh," Navamita said. "She's a magnet for fuckboys, isn't she?"

"That's the impression I'm getting," Bella said. "I think they pedestalize her. They hold her up to this standard that she can never live up to, and whenever she shows her real self, they don't like it. Maybe that's why the relationships don't last. The men and women she dates can't let go of their first impression, which is a fantasy rooted in their own insecurities."

The table was quiet for a moment.

"That was brilliant," Louise said. "How did you come up with that?"

Bella shrugged. "I was thinking about it after last week's session. I guess I have too much time on my hands."

"You should be a writer," Svetlana told her.

Louise gave Chet a nudge. "Write it all down."

Chet blinked, as though in a daze. He didn't seem able to say anything, but he started writing on the worksheet. Bella glanced at him before continuing.

"I was thinking what one of these people might look like. I think the latest one is a man. A man who works with her at the school. Let's call him Ben. Ben teaches maths, but wishes he taught P.E. instead. Even though he's a teacher, he likes to play the class clown. More than anything, he just wants to be noticed, and it probably stems back to when he was a student too."

"Good, good..."

"He likes Aimee because she puts her work out there," Bella continued. Out of the corner of her eye, she noticed the pen pause over the worksheet. "Like Chet said last week, she's kinda shy in person, but her poetry is raw and confessional. Ben used to write too, when he was a student, but he struggles to find the confidence to put his authentic self under the microscope. Happy to joke around in the staff room, an extrovert in fact, but unable to show vulnerability to others. He published a short story at university. About an old clocktower that transports the protagonist to different dimensions, where he can live out alternate versions of his life for a day before returning to his own universe. It was good too, and he wants Aimee to read it, but he's scared."

"Aww!"

"Ben wants Aimee to notice him, but he won't show her the one thing that would pique her interest. So, he continues half-hearted attempts at flirting, all the while idealizing her. But she's just a woman, as flawed and clueless as he is, stumbling her way through life as best she can."

Navamita pouted. "I'm sad. I want them to have a happy ending!"

"As interesting as this is, I think we're straying from the assignment a bit..." Louise said.

Chet didn't speak for the remainder of the seminar. Even the pen-clicking and the chair-rocking had come to a stop. When the seminar was over, their table filed out of the classroom together once again. Louise said goodbye in a businesslike voice and left to join some friends of hers by the water fountain. The four of them descended the stairs, Navamita doing almost all of the talking.

"Look, they have a little bakery set up in the courtyard!" she crooned, linking arms with Svetlana and steering her toward the stall. Laughing, Svetlana called goodbye over her shoulder. Bella and Chet walked in silence through the Main Building before spilling out onto the street. They came to a simultaneous stop by a flowerbed, not knowing which direction the other would be taking.

Chet was the first to speak.

"How'd you find out about that old clocktower story?"

"You're not the only one who knows how to use social media," Bella told him.

Chet nodded. They shared a look and parted ways, Chet heading for the bus stop and Bella to her apartment. When she checked her phone, she noticed a new text message from her grandma.

That would be a Common Starling, sweetie. Gregarious little bugger.

IV

The DM had come as a surprise. The man found the location on Google Maps and followed the directions alongside the river. The Thames at that time of the evening was darker than the sky. A din of faraway conversation floated down the riverfront toward him. The man followed it to a pub called The Ram. He ordered a San Miguel at the bar and began looking for her, sipping as he went.

His search took him to the beer garden that overlooked the river, where he found her sitting at a table in the corner. She didn't exactly smile when she looked at him.

"You came," Aimee stated in a flat voice.

Ben settled himself into the seat opposite her, raising his eyebrows.

"You were expecting otherwise?"

Aimee didn't answer. She gazed in the direction of the Thames and took a heavy draw from her pint.

"Stella," he remarked, nodding at her glass. "I didn't figure you for a beer drinker."

Aimee leveled her eyes at him, and there was the suggestion of a smile in her face.

"No, I guess you didn't," she said, returning the glass to her lips. "How disappointingly on-brand of you."

Aimee kept her eyes on his as she drank. Ben found it difficult to hold her gaze, and he suspected she knew it. He stared instead at the patio, his heart sinking a little at the thought that he would never say the right thing that would secure a connection with her. She would remain unknowable, a kind of walking myth on the periphery of his small universe.

As though sensing this, Aimee said, "I really enjoyed your clocktower story."

"You sound surprised."

"No, it's just, I'm wondering why it took me stalking your Facebook to find out about it."

"I ain't ashamed of it," Ben said. "It meant a lot to me in fact. It's just that it feels like the only good idea I ever had. I've tried writing a whole bunch of stories since, but none of them were worth a damn. Just ran outta steam I reckon. Hence why I became a P.E. teacher."

"Maths teacher," she corrected him.

"Right," he said. They both reached for their beers at the same time, and Ben started to wonder if they might finally be in sync. Aimee looked like she was holding back a smirk as she drank.

"You have a nice turn of phrase. I'm not telling you what to do with it, I'm just saying it's there."

"I'd *like* to do something with it," Ben said. "And thanks, by the way. I tried, for a while. But with every story I tried to write, I started to realize I didn't have anything to say. Not really. I'd rather have good ideas and a crumby turn of phrase than vice versa. I'm someone that wants to tell a story rather than someone who has a story to tell, and I hate that. It's a lousy thing to be."

"Why? Not that I'm agreeing with your assessment of yourself by the way."

"Because it feels like the greats were who they were because they had something important to give the world. Take Steinbeck for example. It feels like he was destined to be who he was, that one way or another, those books were going to get written."

Aimee considered his words as she took another draw of her Stella. Ben realized then that the beer garden at The Ram had actually gotten quite loud, but that talking with Aimee had drowned it out up until now. The night was in full swing. A dozen disconnected conversations blurred around them, seemingly invasive yet affording them total privacy. Walls of sound, with the lives of individual noise-makers bleeding through now and then.

"I know it might seem that way," Aimee replied, placing her beer back on the table. "But what do we know about the greats, really? They're just people at the end of the day. We can't imagine them any other way than they were because their story is already finished. You want to be Steinbeck, do you?"

Ben laughed, blushing. "I don't know."

"Nothing wrong with that," she said.

"Ain't you gonna tell me to just be myself?"

"I don't know you. You might be an arsehole."

"Seemed like you had me figured pretty good the other day," Ben said. Now it was his turn to look her in the eyes. But the effect must not have been the same, because Aimee returned his stare with a blank expression. "Guess I ain't authentic in my writing or my real life."

"Don't be self-pitying, it's unattractive. Why don't you write about Texas?"

"Texas? What's there to write about?"

"No idea, I've never been there. It scares me. But there has to be *something* you can write about it."

Ben thought about it. Her mythic Texas and his lived one. He had a lot to say on it, but he knew that no matter how he worded his response, there was no way to convey the totality of his feelings. All he could do was give her an impression for her imagination to interpret. Language, he realized, was crude and limited. His truth could only ever be known by himself.

Depressing.

"I was born in Hong Kong," Ben said at last. "But we moved to Houston when I was two. So I don't consider myself Chinese in any meaningful way. Sure, I speak Cantonese and my parents are Chinese first and Americans second, but I don't remember anything from Hong Kong. The city is foreign to me. Houston is my home. Texas is what made me who I am."

He paused. They had almost finished their pints. Aimee regarded him with interest, but made no comment, so he continued.

"Not that it mattered. Folks there saw me as Chinese, even though I was as Texan as any of them. And then when the pandemic happened, it only got worse. Felt like I was right back there in elementary school."

Aimee nodded like she understood. Or maybe she was just acknowledging what he said. He had given her the abridged version. A part of him wanted to keep going, but it wouldn't have made much difference, he thought.

"Couldn't you write about that?" Aimee said at last.

"I dunno..." Ben said, scratching his neck. "Felt like growing up, I was defined that way against my will, so I don't want to define myself that way in my writing."

Aimee nodded again. She nursed the pint glass with both hands but didn't drink from it. Instead, she smiled- a new smile, he noted- and nodded in the direction of the Thames.

"You came to the right city," she said.

"Why's that?"

"Everyone here is from somewhere else- whether that's a different part of the U.K. or a different country altogether. Makes it harder to be other-ed."

"You like London, then?"

Aimee laughed.

"That's about the only thing I like about it," she said. "Everything else I hate."

Ben raised his eyebrows.

"I think your Aimee loves the city," she said. "She feels like she's in a movie every time she gets the overground across the Thames or drinks coffee in the park. She definitely exists- she's just not me. I'm only here to take what I need from this city, and as soon as I can I'll peace out."

"What do you need?"

"Same as everyone that comes here. Money. Or education. But you could say those are the same thing, really. This Master's we're doing is the only way we can stand out from all the other job applicants. It sucks, but it's just the way it is."

Ben winced. Nowadays a Bachelor's just didn't cut it.

"I'm just not a city person," Aimee continued. "Or a people-person, to be honest."

"Sure you are," Ben said. "Okay, I don't really know you. But that icebreaker session, the very first week, you told me I had a nice smile."

Aimee's expression softened. Maybe she remembered, he thought, or maybe she just gave out compliments as a matter of habit and thought nothing of it.

"Some people never get complimented," he said. "So it sticks with them forever when it happens."

Ben could see then that she had traced his steps from that one remark to the discovery of her Instagram.

"Well, you do have a nice smile," Aimee said. "So I'm sure I meant it."

There was a pause. Neither of them touched their drinks. Ben could feel his cheeks prickling with warmth, a dryness in his throat. Aimee, for her part, had lost her composure. She seemed loose. Her eyes roamed around the beer garden and he wondered if she now found it less easy to hold his gaze.

"I guess I am a people-person in some ways. You had me dead to rights as an angry feminist. But you were wrong about that underpinning this detached player-lifestyle. I've had the same boyfriend, on-and-off, since school."

"Are you on now or off?" Ben asked.

Aimee grinned at him.

"Why?"

"I was just curious."

"Aimee's story doesn't end with Ben getting laid," she said, and he blushed furiously. Before he could say anything, Aimee continued. "My man lives back in Suffolk. He grew up on the farm opposite ours, and we used to play in the

207

rapeseed field between his place and mine. The on-and-off thing started when we were teenagers- I guess we were still figuring out how to work together- and then during lockdown it just suddenly…calcified."

It was hard for Ben to reconcile his cosmopolitan impression of Aimee with the rural image she had given him. He replaced scenes of her reading *Under the Soil* in cafes with her reading it under a tree. And scenes of her meeting up with unloved strangers in pubs like this one with her walking through the countryside hand-in-hand with a man that probably knew her as well as she knew herself.

"I decided I would stop being cross with him after one beer," Aimee said, holding up the pint to show Ben the little that was left. "Then I'll text him back. I figured I could play Aimee for you while that happens. That's what she does right? Becomes what people need her to be."

"I don't want Aimee," Ben said. "I'm interested in deconstructing the myth."

"Are you?" she countered, setting the glass back down. "Most people aren't."

"What about your boyfriend? Is that why you're mad at him?"

Aimee gave him a short smile- not her real smile, he decided. Not the involuntary one she had let slip a minute ago. "No," she said after a pause. "He sees me as I am. But that doesn't mean everything is perfect all the time. I don't think either of us are truly angry. We're just stressed. Me being in London isn't exactly easy."

Ben nodded. "Makes sense I reckon. Don't let me keep you," he said, gesturing to her beer. "I'll probably hang here for a while."

"I had a nice time talking to you," she said.

"Thanks, you too," Ben said. "Did we finish Aimee and Ben's story then?"

"I think so."

"I don't like endings."

"All things have to end sometime," Aimee said, and gulped the last of her Stella.

V

The two threads came undone, one pushing itself doggedly forward and the other finally submitting to the pull of its past.

The former took comfort in new faces. Weekend trips to Central. An internship at a literary agency. The Kingston University rowing team. A girl named Zahra that studied UX Design and liked board games, especially when she beat him.

The second thread took comfort in old rhythms. Walks through a particular copse of trees she knew like the back of her hand. The dogs that wore themselves out during the day and laid themselves helplessly in her lap come the evening. Substandard Wi-Fi and an old fireplace. Forehead kisses.

Memory of one another dissipated as new problems and curiosities asserted themselves. Poems continued to be written with steadfast regularity. Each week the online engagement increased. Now and then he would read them and the myth would resurface. It was hard not to see every line as a clue, and every poem as a puzzle. But he would not allow himself to slip back into a parasocial relationship, and though he didn't unfollow the account, he began to scroll past the new posts.

On a patio outside a farmhouse, a woman watched her boyfriend shuffling flashcards as he lay in a hammock. It was a light evening and their bellies were full of barbecued sausages and beer they had brewed themselves.

She took a swig of the beer from a glass stein and said, "Hit me."

"Wild animal, lapis lazuli, and tall poppy syndrome," her boyfriend read out.

She nodded, chugging the last of the beer, and letting out a kind of feral growl through her teeth. Within twenty minutes she presented him with a fresh poem in a leather-bound notebook.

"How the fuck do you do that?" he asked.

"Hit me," she said again, pouring herself another beer.

"You're crazy," he told her, but his face was full of admiration. He shuffled the prompts again, grinning.

She studied his face. *God, how completely I love you,* she thought.

At the same time, a hundred miles to the south-west, a man had written his first short story in years. Zahra asked him what he was typing. Reflexively, he said "Oh, just this damn essay."

"I thought you finished that essay."

"I have another one."

They went back to working in silence on the third floor of the Kingston Town House. That night he felt bad. Old habits lingered in his bones. He thought about calling her but decided against it. Instead, he re-read the short story for the dozenth time. His phone buzzed once but he ignored it. The piece was good, but it wasn't pleasant reading. It told the story of a fourteen-year-old boy going on a family trip to China, to visit relatives he had only ever heard about, and being miserable because he was missing a baseball tournament he and his friends had planned that summer. It didn't matter to him how those friends impersonated him behind his back, or how deeply he knew his parents loved him. He was aware of a perverse phenomenon of wanting to please the boys that didn't deserve his devotion and taking a bitter pleasure in disappointing the parents that did.

He opened up Instagram, and sure enough an illustrated poem appeared on his feed, right on time. After reading the first few lines, he jumped up in a flash, and like a man possessed took the last bus that night back to campus. The Town House was almost deserted when he got there. In his coat pocket was a memory stick. He plugged it into the printer and pressed the button that came up on the little rectangular screen.

Sometime after midnight, he arrived outside of Zahra's apartment building.

"It's me," he said into the buzzer.

"Is everything okay?"

"Just wondering if you could read something for me."

VI

When Marta Kushak finally took the stage, a flurry of cellphones shot up in the air and she put on her best smile, glancing up once but careful not to look at them too long. The room was so full that people sat on crossed legs like schoolchildren around the edges. Most of them were older than her.

She maintained the smile and tried not to think about whether she had chosen the right outfit. It was too late now. She had gone for dungarees over a long-sleeved orange top.

Her hair was tied up in a high bun and she gazed at the interviewer through large, silver-rimmed glasses.

The rumble of the crowd subsided and the interviewer began the introduction.

"We are delighted to introduce The 2022 London Book Fair's Author of the Day, Marta Kushak..." the woman was saying. Marta found it hard to concentrate. The phones were still up, even though there would be a whole hour for them to take photos. Behind where she sat, a giant poster showed off various covers of *Under the Soil*, and the breathless interviewer was holding up a copy as she spoke.

It had been almost three years since the book's release, but the public events always felt surreal.

"...coming to Netflix this summer..."

Marta hadn't been happy about the summer release. She had never really thought of it as a summery kind of book. There had been a lot of discussion about what release window suited it best, but ultimately it wasn't up to her.

The novel had become something else once it was published. The words were the same, but no one talked about it the way she had imagined they would when she was writing it. That was her folly, she knew- the assumption that everyone would naturally see it the way she did. But that wasn't necessarily a bad thing, she supposed.

Despite her best efforts, she looked up at the faces of the audience during the interview. All of them were beaming at her- which was sweet- but it agitated the existing imposter syndrome that coiled around her gut.

Some loved the book because it was a love story. Some loved it because it touched on the immigrant experience. Some even saw their own lives in the book. And others didn't care for the book at all, but were there because the name Marta Kushak seemed to mean something important now.

Many of the people in the audience had copies of *Under the Soil* in their laps. Marta braved another glance as she spoke, deciding to focus randomly on one person in the crowd. Her eyes landed on a tall, strong-limbed man leaning against the wall. He wore a denim button-down shirt and black jeans, and she noticed the turquoise of her book in his hand.

Most of her readers were female- another thing she blamed on the marketing department- so she continued to focus on him whenever she lifted her gaze. That would have been something she would have liked to talk about. People decided for you who to sell your book to, to the inevitable exclusion of others. And the books they decided to sell to young women were never taken seriously by critics. They ended up in dust jackets of brilliant turquoise.

When the interview was over, people lined up to get their copies signed. To her delight, the man was among them. A lot of the books she was presented with were dog-eared and lovingly-annotated. When the man passed her his own copy, it looked almost brand new, and a bookmark was placed just over a hundred pages in.

"That was real interesting," the man told her. *An American!* A Southerner by the sounds of it. "I ain't finished your book yet, but I'm digging it so far."

"Thank you," Marta said, making sure her signature had a little extra flair for this one.

"Get it...*digging it*...because it's called *Under the Soil*..."

Marta looked up and the man waggled his eyebrows, grinning at her. She couldn't help it- she burst out laughing. The man seemed relieved.

"Ahem. Sorry. I'd been planning to say that for the past hour."

Marta handed him his signed copy, careful not to let the bookmark slip out.

"You're cute," she said.

As she continued signing copies and obliging a few selfies, Marta noticed the man had approached a woman to her right. It was right in her peripheral vision, in the only free space in the room a conversation could be had. The woman wore a long, flowing black dress with pink spots.

"Howdy stranger," the man said.

"Chet- I mean Ben- how are you?" the woman answered.

Two names?

"Aimee with an E. Doing just swell. Didn't expect to see you here. I thought you dropped out?"

"I didn't drop out. I just decided to go part-time instead. That way I could move back to Suffolk and only come in for Mondays. I guess we have opposite schedules."

"I guess we do. I still read your poems by the way. Seems like your account has really blown up since I last saw you. Congrats."

A poet!

"Thanks. And congrats to you too. I read your new story in the *KU RiPPLE*. You should be proud. That couldn't have been easy to write for you."

Marta couldn't see but she felt like she could somehow hear the man blushing in the pause that followed. She maintained her marketing-smile as she signed the remaining copies, yet her ears strained toward the conversation on her right.

"I appreciate that. Felt like you helped."

"Ah, bollocks," the woman replied.

"I mean it."

"Whatever. I'm proud of you, my little starling."

If the man replied to this peculiar term of endearment, Marta didn't catch it. She tried not to look distracted as she kept up with the signing. Three girls wanted to get a picture with her, and she lost track of the man and the woman. Starting tomorrow, she decided, she would start writing again. She needed to shed the public, marketing-approved Marta Kushak for a while. Starting tomorrow it would just be her fingers and a Word document.

The man and the woman faded from her peripheral vision- but her imagination had all it needed.

The Understudy

The young woman leaned forward, artificial light flashing over her face in the dark room. The news story she was watching depicted a woman giving birth in a Kyiv subway station. The station was packed with masses of people seeking shelter. When the first image of the baby was displayed on the screen, the young woman seemed to instinctively touch her palm to her belly. That the child was born into violence was not obvious from the picture. The young woman stared at a healthy babe with wide, curious eyes and cheeks full of color. Even the blanket was unsoiled, wrapped neatly around the infant body in a cocoon as white as snow.

The young woman watched until the coverage moved onto a different story, whereupon she shut her laptop. When the laptop closed, the bombs and the gunshots and the refugees would be suspended, it seemed, until she opened it again. She sat in the dark, left now in the insular silence of her own life. The silence ended with the rattling of her roommate, Amelie, punching in the key code to their door.

"Hey," Amelie said. Curt, businesslike.

"Did you see that story of the woman giving birth in the Kyiv subway?" the young woman asked.

"Oh, yeah," Amelie said, lifting her backpack off her shoulder with a grimace. "Yeah, I didn't click on it though."

They were silent for a moment. The young woman watched her roommate stretching her back. As she thrust her hips forward, there was an audible popping sound from the base of her spine.

"That better be the last all-nighter I have to do this semester," Amelie grumbled.

The young woman was gazing at Amelie without really focusing on her.

"Do you ever feel like these news stories make your own life feel less real?" the young woman said at last.

"What?"

"Like, they make you feel as though you're not really doing anything. Like you're not living in the real world, the one that everyone sees but few take part in."

Amelie frowned at her. "No. I feel the opposite if anything. If it's not right in front of me, it's hard for me to make sense of it."

The young woman paused for a moment. Then she said, "It's just...I've been going through these cycles. I'll watch the live coverage from Ukraine, until I either get so depressed I turn it off, or I have to go do something- class or whatever. Then, I'll forget about it for a few hours. I'll worry about this paper I'm writing, about groceries, about guys, about my friends. You know, the usual fixations. A video game I'm excited for, a book I'm reading. Shit, anything really. Then I'll check social media and it all comes rushing back, and it hits me hard like I'm seeing it for the first time again. It's shocking, because I realize that while I was doing all that trivial stuff, all those people were still suffering that whole time."

"Stop," Amelie said. "You need to stop that. You'll drive yourself crazy. In fact, you should probably unplug from social media for a while."

"And just pretend it isn't happening?"

"There's *literally* nothing you can do."

The young woman dropped her gaze to her lap. Amelie looked at her for a while longer, before removing her glasses and rubbing her eyes. She changed into her pajamas and climbed into her lofted bed. As Amelie pulled the covers over her chest, the young woman finally snapped into movement.

"Shoot, I have to go," the young woman said, gathering her things. Amelie watched her from her bunk. Morning light crept in through the edges of the blinds.

The young woman was about to head out the door when Amelie sat up. "Hey," she said. "Did you throw up this morning?"

The young woman blushed. "No, no," she said, trying to smile. "I think I'm better now."

"Good. I was getting suspicious."

The young woman forced a laugh and left. The image of the metro baby in its unblemished blanket dissolved, pixel by pixel, from her mind with each step she took down the stairwell of the dorm. The present asserted itself effortlessly. She hurried past the empty volleyball courts and the leafless trees of Upper Campus, careful not to slip on the ice as she made her way down the hill. All around her was cloudless sky. As she made her way with cautious footsteps down the hill toward Lower Campus, the Chippewa River expanded before her into the distance. Dark, shallow, and seemingly unmoving. Gray mounds of waterlogged snow lined the banks.

When she arrived at the red brick façade of Hibbard, the humanities building, the young woman spotted him. It was possible he hadn't noticed her, because he slipped into the building without holding the door open. By now the metro baby was as distant and fictive as an unremembered dream. The young woman grabbed her mask from the back pocket of her jeans and entered the building. She followed the man to a classroom on the third floor but didn't rush to close the distance. When she entered the classroom, a little out of breath, she took the seat directly behind him.

The young woman kept her eyes fixed on the back of the man's head, centered on the little notch in his skull above the neck, where his cropped hair started, richly dark against his skin. Everything else- the excitable chatter of her peers, the zipping and unzipping of bags, the scraping of chair legs on the floor- was white noise.

Even when Professor Chao closed the door behind her and started talking about Maslow's Hierarchy of Needs, the young woman was not listening. Her eyes remained on the short follicles that carpeted that endearing lump of bone, which she knew were not actually black, but the darkest shade of brown.

A sign-in sheet made its way around the room. As the man turned to hand it to her, the young woman felt her heart go aflutter. The man's expression suggested he hadn't expected to find her sitting there. The whole thing must have only lasted a second- but for the young woman, that second carried the weight of nineteen years. Nineteen years, which was the weight of a life that wasn't written about or broadcasted, that didn't touch the real world or was in turn touched by it, that continued unheard in a rhythm all its own.

*

Two babies- one of them expected and the other undetected by the ultrasound- sharing a white blanket. The first baby, Marianne, would have no problem taking their mother's nipple. The second, who for the first day of her life went nameless, had to be fed by bottle. The first, who had clothes waiting for her knitted in her name, slept well. The second, whose clothes were hastily thrifted from the Salvation Army, kept their mother awake all night with piercing cries. But the sight of the two children nestled together underneath that single blanket, their little bodies sharing heat, was the delight of everyone that saw them. It would have been a perfect photo, had it not been for a yellowish discoloration near the top of the blanket. Their mother sighed, explaining that the second child had probably stained it.

The two girls were identical, but Marianne grew up beautiful. New kids at school asked how everyone could tell them apart, and the kids that knew them always answered that it was obvious which one was which. From a distance, no one could tell which of the girls was the obsession of her classmates, whose phone never stopped ringing, whose locker was full of handwritten, heart-signatured notes. But as the girls came into focus, it was clear. One of the girls had an effortless humor that she could strike up with anyone- new kids, grown-ups, shy kids, even total strangers. She made everyone she talked to feel like they were interesting. The other girl, her step an inch behind her sister's, kept her gaze on the ground. She didn't know how to talk to other people and they didn't know how to talk to her.

To the second child, who spent much of her time in the full-length mirror of her closet, the differences were very obvious. Her skin was deathly pale, she had none of Marianne's curves, her lips were thin. Then there were differences, not of her body, but in how it behaved: the restless eyes, the fidgeting hands, the lopsided poses, the quiet monotone in which she spoke.

To her, the machine of their mother's uterus had meant to print two perfect copies, but had suffered a glitch producing the second one. The subtle kind that you only noticed when you got home. A lack of symmetry and smoothness. A less saturated print.

Every boy that met Marianne fell in love with her, and the second child hated every one of them. The boy Marianne liked best lived down the road, on a soybean farm. A quiet, all-state wrestler with workaholic parents and no siblings. When they were fourteen, Marianne dragged her sister over to his house where the three of them would have free reign for the whole day. Jumping on the trampoline would always end with the second child watching the two of them exhaust each other in a tickling match. Marianne breathless, eyelashes catching the sun.

One day, when Marianne was sick, they stayed home. The second child was reading on the front porch when she noticed the boy cycling up their driveway. There was no traffic and no breeze, just the pine needles snapping beneath his approach.

"Marianne's sick today," she told him in a flat voice.

"Sorry to hear that," the boy said. The young girl waited for him to turn and leave, but he stood where he was, smiling up at her. He had a big jaw and a face that always looked like it was holding back mocking laughter. The young girl glared down at him.

"So, we're not coming over today."

The boy smiled, though it was really more of a smirk.

"What do you want?" the young girl snapped.

"*You're* not sick, are you?"

"No."

"I came to see you."

The young girl laughed.

"What's so funny?"

"Fuck off," she told him, returning to her book.

"I'm serious. You're my favorite twin," he said. The young girl cocked her head at him, though she trembled despite herself. To hide this fact, she set her book down on the table.

"What part of *fuck off* don't you understand?"

"You said you're not sick. Go get your bike, we can play on the trampoline."

The young girl didn't say anything. She imagined the boy tickling her on the trampoline the way he always did Marianne. As though sensing this, the boy's smirk became a wide grin. He started up the steps of the porch, but then his eyes flicked toward something over her shoulder. The girl turned around just in time to see the blinds swing back into place.

"You should go," the young girl said. The boy looked disappointed. The young girl was disappointed too.

That summer, the boy's family sold their farm and moved to Oshkosh. Sometimes his stupid face would pop up in the second child's dreams. That she continued to dream about him years after he left amused her.

In 2020 the girls turned seventeen, but only one of them would turn eighteen. That anything could be faulty with Marianne shocked the second child. The doctors suspected an undiagnosed heart condition that made her especially vulnerable to the virus. There was a tiny funeral, with extended family joining via Zoom, that in no way matched the immensity of Marianne's life. The second child would go for a test weeks later to see if she had the same heart defect, and somehow the result came back negative. She wondered if she had had the virus without knowing it, that it had been her that had taken Marianne from the world that loved her. Her parents must have thought the same thing. Sharing a room like that.

It should have been the other way around, the second child thought. Lose the understudy, if you're going to lose anyone. Her parents probably thought that too. Her mother's uterus screaming: *that's what the backup was there for!*

During the boredom of the pandemic, the second child would try on Marianne's clothes in the full-length mirror. Cute, strappy dresses and summery colors. Things that she had never tried to pull off. When her parents caught her wearing them, they screamed at her and threw all of the clothes in the garbage. The second child knew that it was difficult for them to look at her, that it probably always would be from now on. The understudy had become the ghost. College couldn't come soon enough for all of them.

College. A haze of midnight pizza and basement beer pong. River tubing and hipster cafes in the brick remnants of an old logging town. A roommate for a new sister. A fresh blanket for a soiled one.

At first, the second child felt guilty about how happy her new life made her. The people she met in the pickup volleyball games that first week were all untouched by Marianne's grace. When they smiled at her across the net, they saw only her. Every time they called her name, it was the sweetest thing her ears had ever received. That semester she didn't visit home once, and when she went back for Christmas, she couldn't wait for January to come around.

January. A game of indoor intramural soccer. His face hadn't changed. It still looked like it was on the verge of laughter. Their eyes met after her shot went through his legs and lashed the back of the net. He smiled. She smiled back. The boy- now a man- was clumsy at soccer. Too top-heavy, not used to using his feet. Probably thought he could bulldoze his way through it. A fool, she thought, but the only person from home who had ever really looked at her.

After the game, they walked up to each other. She waited for him to say her name- her favorite sound.

"Well, well," he said, grinning at her. "If it isn't Marianne..."

It took a while for his mistake to register. He must have mistaken her pause for being out of breath from the game. The young woman panted, hands on hips, and offered a smile. The window to correct him was fast closing. It hadn't occurred to her that he wouldn't know.

Before she could even answer, the man invited her to a frat party that same night. The young woman managed a nod. Maybe his assumption made sense, having seen her laughing at one of Amelie's racy jokes, the high-fives of her teammates. Just the fact she was playing sports. The man probably had no memory of her smiling.

As she opened her closet back in her room, she wondered if she could do it. *If he wants Marianne, I can be Marianne for him,* she told herself. *No one studied her better.*

When she spotted him through the dancing bodies, she put on her best Marianne-smile and started towards him. Teeth showing, shoulders back. Open body language. And laugh. Laugh a lot. He asked her later how her twin sister was doing, and the young woman replied "Thriving, actually."

That night his hot breath was in her ear. With her arms slung under his armpits, she gripped his shoulders, pulling him deeper. Right up until he finished, he panted her sister's name. That he hadn't been able to stop himself in time did not surprise her. When he caressed her bottom lip with his thumb, the young woman knew for the first time in her life what it was truly like to be Marianne. The care- the *deference-* in his fingertips, as though he couldn't believe his luck.

*

The man turned quickly back to Professor Chao's slides, and the second child went back to staring at the notch in his head. She had no doubt that, for him, that second had only lasted a second.

Once the class was over, she followed him outside, down the stairwell, across the sidewalk, and up the steps to the footbridge. Wintry leftovers crumpled into the shallow water below. When he was almost exactly halfway across the Chippewa footbridge, the man spun around on his heel, his lips twisted into something like a snarl.

"I told you to stay away."

"Please," the young woman whimpered.

"That was really fucked up, what you did," the man growled at her. "You need fucking psychiatric help."

The young woman started crying. The man sighed, but kept his distance from her.

"Okay, I shouldn't have yelled like that," he said. "But if you want to make this right, then please, never, *ever*, speak to me again."

A cold wind blew down the river, whipping their faces. The young woman let him go. She remained on the footbridge for a while, until, feeling the chill in her bones, she started back the other way. Past the jacketed bodies, hands in their pockets. Past Little Niagara, that snaked delicately through Lower Campus and spilled into the Chippewa. Past trees that would soon be full of color.

Her own life contracted behind her, and as she opened her laptop, the world opened with it.

Acknowledgements

First and foremost, I would like to extend my heartfelt thanks to Professor Emma Tait for guiding me through the world of publishing under her wing. Your mentorship has been an integral part of this book from its inception to its final release. I'm in awe of your uncanny ability to look at a book and within a split second be able to dissect its various strengths and weaknesses, providing specific and actionable suggestions for how to improve it.

I would also like to give special thanks to Professors Alison Baverstock, Lucy Upton, and Clare Somerville for their invaluable wisdom over the past academic year. And I would like to give particular thanks to the late Dan Newman for teaching me the fundamentals of book design, without which this project wouldn't have been possible.

To my parents, Ian and Meryl Vowles, I offer my eternal gratitude. Thank you for the tools, for the conditions, and for your tireless support toward everything I undertake.

Thank you to my brother, Andrew Vowles, for giving me the courage to make this book a reality. Were it not for your determination to see me become the best version of myself, I would never have moved to London in the first place, and this book simply never would have gotten started. Without you, there would be nothing.

I would like to thank my good friend Jacob Radka, whose thorough proofreading and creative advice helped see this book over the finishing line. Thanks are also in order for my wonderful friends Brittany Radka, Meghan Begley, and Toby Hale for all their support throughout this project- I couldn't have done it without your dogged belief in me.

Thank you to Marisa Spence for providing me with an excellent set of author photos- it was so fun shooting with you on the rooftop of the Kingston University Town House.

Last- but certainly not least- I would like to reserve my deepest thanks for my friend Jasmine S. Higgins; cover designer, illustrator, proofreader, consultant, and confidante. No one knew Fractured Threads more intimately than you during its development, throughout which you showed as much passion for it as you did your own book. Without those countless writing sessions we had at The Press Room in Surbiton, this book would look very different. Thank you for everything- especially for designing and illustrating a cover that reflects so well what *Fractured Threads* is all about. I'm constantly in awe of your talent and I can't wait for our next collaboration.

Lightning Source UK Ltd.
Milton Keynes UK
UKHW012238250822
407863UK00003B/39

9 781399 932219